Christmas

Through

the Years

A War Cry Collection

Selected from the official national publication
of The Salvation Army in the USA from
issues beginning 1947 to the present

Crest Books

Salvation Army National Publications
615 Slaters Lane
Alexandria, Virginia 22313

Published by Crest Books
The Salvation Army National Publications
615 Slaters Lane
Alexandria, VA 22313

ISBN 0-9657601-1-1

Library of Congress Catalog Card Number: 97-69055

Unless otherwise indicated, all scripture references are from the King James Version.

Scripture noted NIV is taken from the HOLY BIBLE, NEW INTERNATIONAL VERSION. Copyright © 1973, 1978, 1984 International Bible Society. Used by permission of Zondervan Bible Publishers.

Printed in the United States of America.

Cover art, first appearing in *The War Cry*, 1991, by Karen Yee Lim.

Contents

4

Foreword

Christmas Through the Years is a treasury of articles, stories, poetry and art from Christmas issues of *The War Cry* over the past fifty years. Some of us have clear memories of those earliest contributors. Others are more familiar with recent writers and artists. Regardless of the generation, the timeless Christmas message is consistently and convincingly presented, and continues to speak to man's deepest needs.

Some of these "treasures" were carried in *The War Cry* as it was distributed by faithful workers at Christmas kettles on cold street corners. In other cases, devoted League of Mercy workers "brightened the corners" of sick and elderly people in hospitals and nursing homes. Some articles penetrated the spiritual darkness of prison cells, as indicated to me recently by a former Dallas inmate, who testified to the impact of *The War Cry* on his life.

Whatever the circumstance or year, doubtless every classic treasure in this volume has ministered Christmas grace to the hearts of people. And that, after all, is the purpose of every issue of *The War Cry*.

As thousands of copies of this volume get into the hands of people across America and around the world, it is our prayer that the gospel it contains will also get into their hearts.

Nearly two thousand years have passed since the birth of Jesus in a lowly Bethlehem stable. He was "the Word made flesh who dwelt among us." As we approach a new millennium, He still dwells among us, and wants to live in the hearts of men and women and boys and girls.

The Salvation Army is still in the business of getting that wonderful news to as many as possible. May all who read this volume get the message that changes lives.

May God bless you with the spirit of Christmas throughout the year!

Commissioner Robert A. Watson
National Commander

Acknowledgments

Christmas Through the Years is the achievement of many individuals—writers, editors, artists, designers, technicians and production specialists. Each, working to the honor and glory of God, has made this volume possible, but Crest Books pays special tribute to the editors-in-chief who directed national and territorial editions of *The War Cry* over the past 50 years:

Vincent Cunningham, (South) 1933-1951
Rowland Hughes, (Eastern) 1940-1964
R. Lewis Keeler, (Central) 1941-1964
Connie Sly, (West) 1947-1948
Muriel Creighton, (West) 1949-1956
Lillian Hansen, (South) 1952-1969
Kathleen McClelland, (West) 1957-1969
Robert Thomson, (Central) 1965-1966, (National) 1970-1971
Ralph Miller, (East) 1965-1966, (National) 1979-1980
Donald Rose, (Central) 1967-1968
William Barr, (East) 1967-1969
Alvern Ericson, (Central) 1969
Alfred Gilliard, (National) 1967-1969
William Burrows, (National) 1972-1978
Henry Gariepy, (National) 1980-1994
Marlene Chase, (National) 1995-present

National Publications also recognizes managing editor Jeffrey S. McDonald, whose Christmas prayer appears on the final page. For 13 years, he has edited the Christmas, Easter and regular editions of *The War Cry* with skillful dedication.

Christmas Eve Prayer

Colonel P.L. DeBevoise
1959

Dear God: We hate to bother You on the eve of Your Son's birthday. But He isn't a Baby in the manger any more. He's grown up now and is our Savior. We know that for His sake You'll take time out and listen to what's on our hearts.

Mind You, we've no complaints. We feel good. We've got friends, food, colored lights with bubbles in them and a pile of packages wrapped in fancy paper and tied with pretty ribbons. And the old Christmas sparkle is in our hearts.

But what worries us is those folks who may not feel Christmasy tomorrow. Can You do something to help them?

We mean folks who have to work on Christmas Day. Take policemen, firemen, mechanics, electricians, stokers down at the town power plant. What would we do if they refused to work on the Lord's birthday? Couldn't You tell them somehow that we're praying for them, hoping the malcontents will behave, that fir trees won't catch fire and fuses will burn out some other day than Christmas?

We're sorry for telephone operators who must plug in long-distance calls for everybody's mother except their own. And we pray for waitresses, who must be nice to demanding, turkey-filled customers, radio and TV girls who will spend Christmas singing commercial ditties to make their media profitable even on America's number one holiday, disc jockeys who, for our pleasure, keep the tables turning all day with carols.

Then there are cooks, janitors, clerks, bellhops, elevator operators in hotels and apartment houses. They have to stand on duty Christmas Day, with no chance to play games, have fun, eat big and rest lots as we do.

And the reporters who have to meet Christmas deadlines, linotype operators, pressmen, teamsters who make it possible for us to have the newspaper on the morning after Christmas. They really need a big lift as they tiredly make their way home Christmas night.

We think, too, of college students who can't afford to go home to Mom and Pop for the holidays. Sure, they put up a bluff, a brave facade. They try to play at hero. But, God, You see them alone when moisture glistens the eyelashes, just at the thought of the place Dad is proud to support, Ma is glad to keep clean and where the kids like to be, especially at Christmas.

Then there come to mind our sometimes-forgotten protectors, brave sentinels at the outposts of liberty somewhere along the distant Dewline, in the merciless tropics or the biting arctics. Or maybe grim airmen whizzing faster than sound above the tumbling mirth of sun-split clouds. They all have a fierce yet tender yearning for a place called home, that spiritual something that doesn't come in "K" rations, cans or cellophane. Do reach a hand to our fine boys.

Help the parents who, with quivering lips, spend their first Christmas alone, missing the laughter of sons and daughters who have grown up and gone away.

Comfort the mother who hears only in her broken heart the patter of running feet on Christmas morning. All that is left of a pretty dream is memory—a doll, a tricycle, a sled, little shoes that no feet ever wear.

And the widow, pain stabbing at her heart, the breadwinner gone, dadless children clinging to her skirts, an inescapable, nameless dread gripping her. Heal her sleepless scars.

The widower, too, in poignant desolation, vainly trying to join the children in gaiety while his heart is in the shadows. He misses the warm hand, the petite step, the gentle pressure of a kiss, the undying affection he was used to.

And please look the way of orphans. Some are solitary stragglers, others impersonal in regimentation, but all with no mother to hug them tight, no smell of chestnut dressing in the kitchen, no peppermint candy to suck. They're so pitiful, parentless, alone.

Then there are good people behind curtains: bamboo, iron, other kinds. It's a comfort to know that many years ago You took the curtain of the Temple and tore it in two. You can do that again! No tyrants can keep Your blessed presence out of a land where people seem insulated in living silence. May Christmas soon be more than just a memory to all of them.

And displaced persons of whatever race, loved ones torn from their arms, living amidst the crackling of rifle fire even in Jesus' own neighborhood. Let the Bethlehem star break up their night.

We almost forgot the faithful in hospitals—doctors, interns, nurses, those gracious girls of the silent service, dressed in antiseptic white. Even on His natal day they practice the ritual of an alcohol rubdown, change bed sheets, make the sick as comfortable as possible.

Bless dear, lonely old folks, many of them unloved, unwanted, friendless—pensioners who live on a pittance in drab surroundings, thoughts of a dread future coldly encircling the heart.

How we'd like to help You do something for the chain of shuffling, homeless men who go alone, men who one time were little boys, whose parents loved them as we love our own. Yes, God, be kind to men who walk alone.

And men, women, even youngsters, in jails and prisons, paying the penalty of law violation, clutching broken pieces of what once was a lovely ideal. Now their tomorrow seems too frightening and bleak. Whisper to them the words of the wise man who wrote, "Out of prison He cometh to reign."

We pray for all that fraternity of the friendless and unremembered, who, like the Ancient Mariner, feel terribly
> Alone, alone, all alone,
> Alone on a wide, wide sea.

Dear Father, we haven't got columns enough to list them all. But You have them, every one, in Your heart. And if somehow You could get them to read the promise, "God brings the lonely home," well, it would help. That's what men yearn for at Christmas time—home. And You told us that God is our Home in all the ages.

Now, this has been sort of a garbled prayer. But You know what we're trying to say. Please put the words in right order, add the names we've left out, and then we'll go to dinner.

But as we accept of Your bounty, please give us the grace of cheerful consent in sharing the fine things we enjoy with those whose lives are starless heavens or in selfishness we may find that our food chokes us and in callousness we may discover that our blessings have turned sour.

Then, on the day after Christmas, let us go back to the busy days and crowded ways, joining our hands and Yours in putting stars back into the heavens of folks.

In the strong name of our living Lord we ask these things on Christmas Eve. Amen.

No Fear!

General Paul A. Rader
1994

Fear is rife among our young people. Teens fear they might be pregnant—and alone. Teens fear they may have contracted AIDS. Teens fear they may be mugged in the hallways of their schools. Teens fear their families are falling apart. Teens fear their global home is disintegrating into ecological disaster. Teens fear they will be shot in the streets. Teens fear their whole lives will be as boring and purposeless as their present existence. Teens fear they will never know their parents' approval.

They are not alone. Their parents have their own fears—economic failure, family failure, joblessness, homelessness, ill health, redundancy, rejection, racism. Some are paralyzed with anxiety over the threat of natural disaster—earthquake, flood and fire. Others fear being physically assaulted—too often by their own spouses in an epidemic of domestic violence that is a national shame.

In many of our cities, families have been driven by fear to make virtual military redoubts of their own homes. Fear is responsible for a major movement in America toward what trendspotter Faith Popcorn calls "cocooning"—a hunkering down in homes made safe and garrisoned against the hostile world that surrounds us.

After the atrocities of Bosnia, Rwanda and Haiti, what next? Does North Korea have the bomb? The possibility of global disaster darkens the human horizon. But mostly, fear is centered in our troubled selves. And it is to us that the message of Christmas rings out: "No fear!"

Last year, during the flood of the century in the Midwest, many will remember the striking photo of a home surrounded by surging flood waters, on the roof of which the brave family had spelled out in sandbags the words, "No fear." How often we have felt the swelling floodtide of uncontrollable circumstances that threaten to swamp us and destroy all we hold dear. Who then can say, "No fear"?

It is to us in this troubled and anxious age, as in the first century, that the message of the herald angels is given, "Fear not! For unto you is born this day in the city of David a Savior who is Christ the Lord!"

The power of that promise of peace is its grounding in reality. Christmas is not an exercise in nostalgia—a kind of annual tryst with the myths and fables of our childhood, to pluck up one's spirits, like whistling in the dark. Christmas is not an escape from reality. Christmas is reality! The possibility and promise of a "no fear" existence lies in a real Person whose coming frees us from bondage to fear. "Unto you," announced the angels, is this Savior come. His coming is to set us free—all who will open their hearts to His peace.

He came at a particular time—"this day." He came to a particular, identifiable place—"the city of David"—Bethlehem, located just a few miles south of Jerusalem. On this day in this place He did not merely appear. He was born in the pain and blood of His young mother, virgin though she was. "Conceived by the Holy Spirit, born of the Virgin Mary," Christians around the world affirm in the words of the Apostles' Creed. "Since the children have flesh and blood, He [Jesus] too

shared in their humanity so that by His death He might destroy him who holds the power of death—that is, the devil—and free those who all their lives were held in slavery by their fear of death" (Heb. 2:14-15, NIV). That is the Christmas promise—"No fear!"

> *Christ whose glory fills the skies,*
> *Christ, the true, the only light,*
> *Sun of righteousness arise,*
> *Triumph o'er the shades of night;*
> *Dayspring from on high, be near;*
> *Dayspring, in my heart appear.*
>
> *Visit, then, this soul of mine,*
> *Pierce the gloom of sin and grief;*
> *Fill me, Radiance divine,*
> *Scatter all my unbelief;*
> *More and more thyself display,*
> *Shining to the perfect day.*

Perhaps we should all add this hymn by Charles Wesley to our list of favorite carols, for its message is the Christmas message. It can be your prayer this Christmas.

What do you fear? Failure? Future? Futility? Physical suffering? Death? Christ came to save us from our crippling fears by the light of His love and the reality of His presence to all who will in simple faith trust Him as Savior and Lord.

"No fear." It is God's promise to you—wrapped in the reality of His Son, born among us, for us, here and now.

Beyond the Burning

Lt. Colonel Marlene Chase
1996

Joy watched the pine logs burn side by side in the grate. Soft sighing sounds emerged, as though the two logs were gauging time, lest one should burn more quickly than the other. With a kind of morbid fascination she wondered if one might be left to grow cold alone.

It was nearly Christmas and, for the first time in all the years she could remember, there was no tree in the living room, no red and green decorations artfully placed. Even the creche that had

always signaled Advent in their home lay hidden inside its box near the mantle.

It hadn't been a conscious decision, really. But after all, there was no one but her this year. Harold had passed away suddenly one cruelly brilliant day in July. And Janie had wed Martin Crane and gone on an extended trip to Australia. They would not be back until spring, and then perhaps only for a visit.

Jessica was finishing a term at the University in Edinburgh and would spend a late Christmas with Mom in mid-January. So three days before Christmas Joy was all alone. Dreadfully alone.

She could have gone to her brother's in Colorado, but in some strange way she might feel even more alone. At least here she and Harold had been together—like two logs blazing companionably in growing old age.

She frowned into the mirror above the fireplace. Old age? At 50? Really? There was still a certain comeliness about her hazel eyes and chestnut hair only mildly touched with strands of gray.

She turned away, suddenly tired and frightened by her uncharacteristic gloom. She thought she had worked through all that pain in the difficult months past. Friends had been supportive, good.

She stooped to loosen the twine around the box that held the creche. As she lifted it out, she remembered how much she had been helped, how much kindness had come to her.

So what was wrong with her? Maybe it was the pressure at work. Dismally, she glanced in the direction of the coffee table. A thick folder lay at a haphazard angle where she had thrown it a little while earlier. Hank Collier used to be a such a generous, kind employer—even giving her extra time off after Harold's death. But lately, he'd turned into some kind of ogre, taciturn and demanding.

Imagine asking for that extensive research data at 3 o'clock on Friday afternoon—especially at the holiday season when everyone had so much to do! Or perhaps he thought single women didn't need time to bake cookies or wrap gifts, or ... She'd only begun to learn how difficult the single life could sometimes be.

Well, she'd told Hank he'd have to wait—at least until Monday. She had not said it very kindly. Nor had he understood or even responded. He had looked at her with those little muscles in his jaw working, then turned on his patent-leathered heel and left the room.

"Joy to the World," she said to the image in the mirror, sensing the cruel irony of her name. She took the file to her workroom. Why not? There was nothing else to do but stare at the logs in the fireplace.

When the project was finished she got into her car, only mildly aware that a light snow was falling and that she hadn't taken the time for supper. She'd deliver the material so Hank could have his Saturday meeting—or do whatever he planned with the file.

The Collier home on the outskirts of town was a handsome one. His father had lived there before him—and perhaps his father's father too, who had been something of a real estate magnate in that part of the country. It certainly looked like he could afford to hire one more secretary to help with the workload. She slammed the car door, surprised by the angry noise it made.

They would probably be gathered around a fire. The children would be sitting near the tree, dreaming perhaps. Joy knocked too loudly, wondering about the loneliness plaguing her now. Wondering if it was burning out of control.

She knocked. But there was no response. Strange. She could hear a television going, and lights were blazing from the windows. Irritated, she moved around to the rear of the house. The least they could do was answer after all the extra work she'd put in.

She pressed her face against the back window. Suddenly she saw flames rising from the stove! She banged against the glass, then at the back door. Someone had obviously turned the stove up too high under a large frying pan.

A little boy streaked into the room. Then a girl, maybe 12 or so, with long dark hair streamed behind him. She put both hands to her mouth as she drew near the stove, then backed up, screaming. Joy pushed against the door with all her weight, and suddenly she was inside the room.

"The flour! Where's the flour!" she yelled. Instinctively she grabbed the largest canister on the counter near the stove and threw its entire contents over the flames.

A thunk and a hissing, and the flames became a smoking, sticky mess. Joy turned to see the young girl white as the flour and shivering against the kitchen wall. The boy whimpering in the doorway ran to his sister and clung to her blue-jeaned knees.

"It's all right," Joy said gently. She put an arm around the girl's shoulders. "I'm Joy Nelson. I work for your father. I'm so glad you're all right."

The girl nodded and sniffed. "Thank—thank you," she stammered.

"Are you alone here? Where's your mother?"

"She's—sick. She's—in the hospital and Daddy—"

At that point Hank Collier rushed into the kitchen, snowflakes clinging to his hair and coat.

"Oh, Daddy!" The girl rushed to her father, who held her against his chest while his eyes searched Joy's for an explanation.

"I came to deliver the research data—the project I told you I couldn't do. I saw the grease fire from the window." She paused, seeing the mixture of pain and relief on her employer's face. Strange, she hadn't noticed those lines of worry before.

Hank Collier shook his head as he released his young daughter. "I'm very grateful," he said slowly. "I—I—had to leave the children to visit Mary. My wife—" His words broke off, and he dropped down in a kitchen chair.

"Oh, Hank. I'm so sorry. I wish I had known. I would have been glad to help." Suddenly she was ashamed of herself. She should have guessed something had been worrying him. But she hadn't been able to see beyond herself.

She began cleaning up the mess on the stove. Jenny helped, scraping flour into a paper bag, while Hank Collier consoled the little boy on his knee.

"We had hoped Mary would be home for Christmas, but it looks like it won't happen for awhile yet." He looked off somewhere into space as he spoke, and his voice was heavy with sadness.

"Daddy, can we get our Christmas tree now? Can we?" The child pulled impetuously at his daddy's face.

Hank sighed deeply, his blue eyes closing briefly in concentration, or maybe in desperate prayer.

"Why not let me help? I could take the children shopping. I—know how difficult it must have been for you." She paused, noticing for the first time how young and vulnerable he seemed. He was wearing mismatched socks—one navy blue with ribs and the other smooth and black. She smiled, hoping he understood how sorry she was for her earlier lack of understanding.

"I know I owe you an apology," he said in a low, weary voice. "You—and everybody else in the office. I guess I let my problems get the upper hand and I—"

"Believe me, I understand. Listen," she began gently. "I have a freezer full of Christmas cookies that I baked out of habit. But now I don't know what to do with them."

"Do you got any gingerbread men?" the little boy asked with wide eyes.

"The biggest gingerbread men with the most frosting you ever saw," she said, feeling the wonderment of Christmas like a meteor rising in her soul. And to think she had almost let it all pass her by, like so much smoke. Beyond the burning of her own grief she had finally felt the pain of another. Strange what warmth and light were touched off in the shared flame.

Fetch the Major!

Commissioner Will Pratt
1983

I was eleven years old when my officer-parents were appointed in charge of a Salvation Army corps at the heart of grimy old Manchester in industrial England.

They called the area where we lived "All Saints." No wonder! You had to be one to live there. Street cars—steel throated monsters running on rails sunk into the roadway—rattled and bashed their way past our front doorstep from dawn till well after midnight. My mother, born and bred amid the lush green countryside of Cornwall in southwest England, fought a losing battle with the soot that showered down upon her white lace drapes from the common lodging houses opposite.

Our three-story quarters, with dank, dark, cavernous cellar below, was tightly sandwiched between one of Manchester's dark satanic cotton mills on one side and the Salvation Army hall on the other. Our left-hand wall would reverberate with the ceaseless thump of clattering looms. Our right-hand wall would syncopate to the oompah, oompah of senior and young people's brass bands rehearsing their gospel melodies designed to save the world.

As an eleven-year-old boy I quickly discovered the advantages of living next door to the hall. One moment I could be late lying abed. In next to no time I could be fully clothed, if not in my right mind, attending morning Sunday school.

My poor father quickly discovered the disadvantages of living right next door to the Salvation Army hall. Whenever anything was wanted by the industrious but sometimes forgetful Salvationists, they would immediately ring the quarters doorbell.

Tea, milk, sugar, soap, a spare tambourine? "Go and ask the major."

Fuses, matches, candles when the electricity failed? "Go and ask the major."

With seemingly infinite patience my father made no protest. Were not Salvation Army majors ordained by God to provide sugar, soap, matches, fuse wire?

He preferred those requests to the more demanding occasions when some ruffian in that down-at-heel area would walk into the hall and threaten trouble. Then, far more urgently the Salvationists would say "Fetch the major."

Or even those times when his zealous workers would let their quick tempers and strong passions set aside the grace of God and there would be fierce discord among them. Then still more urgently the message would come: "Fetch the major."

At such times my father's patience and never-failing sense of humor did not let him down.

One year, close to Christmastime, feeling utterly exhausted through extra heavy work and preparation, Father resolved to go to bed early. "And they'd better not disturb me tonight," he growled ominously as he made his weary way up the stairs at the unusually early hour of 9:30.

"They" were the bandsmen and other workers who were painting the scenery and putting up the drapes and curtains for the Nativity play organized every year by Jim Redhead. Folk traveled from miles around to see Jim Redhead's plays. Jim was a fine fellow. You could trust Jim to handle anything. Father felt that his good night's sleep was assured.

Alas, his head had hardly touched the pillow when the doorbell rang. With a weariness beyond description he put on his old red dressing-gown and went to the door.

Young Willy Pritchard stood there. Seventeen years old, Willy did not need extrasensory perception to detect that he was not really welcome.

"What is it?" growled Father in a tone that would have done credit to Scrooge.

"P-p-please, Major," stammered Willy in his nervousness. "Jim Redhead said, would I fetch the major."

Sudden totally unaccustomed anger filled my father. He sped back upstairs like an Olympic sprinter, pulled navy serge trousers over protesting pajamas, grabbed his tunic and, not stopping to comb his tousled hair, rushed out of the house, slamming the door behind him. "I'll tell them this time. I'll tell them this time," he muttered.

Still at breakneck speed, he rushed into the hall and like an Old Testament prophet roared. "What is it this time? What on earth do you want me for at this time of night?"

The good Jim Redhead stopped sawing a plank of wood and a look of astonishment spread over his honest face. "I don't understand," he began, but his voice petered out in aba-aba sounds.

Father swung round with accusing finger to the cowering Willy Pritchard. That young man found his voice. "B-b-but you told me, Mr. Redhead, you told me to fetch the major."

There was a moment of silence which seemed like eternity. Slowly Jim Redhead buckled at the knees and sank to the floor. Gurgling noises came from his throat as he spluttered for words and choked with laughter.

"Willy, oh Willy, you got it wrong I didn't say, 'Fetch the major.' I said, 'Fetch the MANGER!'"

We four kids teased Dad for weeks afterward, but actually, young Willy Pritchard wasn't really far wrong when he fetched my dad that night. All his life as a corps officer, Father was dedicated to bringing the manger into people's lives, trying to get men and women to understand what the Bethlehem manger tells us about God.

The manger tells us that though God is so high and holy, He is also so very lowly. Had we been asked to select a place where the Son of God should be born we would have thought of the White House or Buckingham Palace. God chose a crude and drafty stable, lacking every single piece of equipment and sanitation we would have thought essential. The manger compels us to realize with astonishment that there is no situation in life so desolate, so crude, so lowly that God cannot be there.

The manger tells us that when you seek the Babe of the Manger all class distinctions disappear. Humble loving shepherds and wondering wise men found themselves equally at home when they bowed in awe before the manger bed. It's the same today. Colonel Edward Joy's book, *The Old Corps*, tells us that dirty Jimmy and Lady Beatrice could kneel side by side at the Salvation Army penitent-form because they were both seeking the same Lord.

The manger tells us that God is utterly involved in the reality of human affairs. The Son of God could have descended from heaven's glory in a chariot of fire or on a golden throne with angels dancing in attendance. Instead God chose the pain, the tension, the hushed privacy of natural human birth. Everything about our supernatural God is natural when He deals with us. He so wants to be involved in the ordinary affairs of your life and mine.

Amid the tinsel and glitter of so much superficial seasonal celebration this Christmas, I shall seek those moments when very deliberately I fetch the manger yet again into my life, and bow before the sacred baby Boy whose loving nature it so comprehensively reveals.

The Kettle that Boils Around the World

June Alder
1955

Nearly everyone is familiar with the sight of the little red kettle attended by a bell-ringing Salvationist. It's as much a part of the holiday scene as whimsically decorated store windows and street-corner Christmas tree lots.

In almost every city and town across the nation some type of "kettle" boils at Christmas time. In small Midwest prairie towns, on the San Francisco waterfront, on the slushy streets of New York City you'll find the Army's red kettle. The weather may vary from biting, below-zero temperatures of New England to the heat of a Florida resort—but the Salvationist will be there.

For more than half a century The Salvation Army has been collecting funds for its holiday cheer program through varying adaptations of the Christmas kettle device.

It all started in San Francisco back in 1894 when the country was hard hit by a bitter depression. Things were bad in San Francisco. Shipping was practically at a standstill, and hundreds of seamen and longshoremen were out of work.

It was the responsibility of Captain Joseph McFee—himself a seaman before he joined The Salvation Army—to do something to help these men. Taking care of the initial cost, his commanding officer, the late Commissioner William A. McIntyre, instructed him to set up a soup kitchen and shelter. But McFee had to get the money to operate the program.

McFee roamed San Francisco's waterfront asking for donations—with little success. Then one gloomy, wet day, shortly before Christmas, he wandered by a ship chandler's store, a shop where ship's provisions are sold. A huge, black, iron pot hung from a tripod in the window.

An idea clicked in McFee's mind. He bought the pot and tripod on the spot and set it up at the entrance of the Oakland and Alameda ferries at the foot of Market Street. Over it he put a sign: "Keep the pot boiling."

"Help feed the hungry sailors!" McFee called to the crowds passing by. Commuters caught the captain's spirit and soon coins began to clink into the pot. Hungry sailors were fed and The Salvation Army's first Christmas kettle had come into being.

The idea soon spread. The *Sacramento Bee* of December 24, 1895, described the Army's Christmas activities and mentioned the contributions to "street corner kettles."

By 1900 the device was used across the nation. In 1898 the *New York World* printed a story about the Salvation Army kettle, calling it "the newest and most novel device for collecting money."

"It has met with remarkable success because it has struck popular fancy," the paper said. "It is an iron boilingpot such as is used in every household, suspended from a tripod of red sticks about the height of a man. The inscription, 'Keep the pot boiling,' leaves no doubt of its object. There is a man in charge to see that contributions are not stolen. It is much more effective than personal solicitation. The fact that there is no importunity causes many to contribute who otherwise

16

would refuse."

Today in most cities the contributions dropped in the kettles finance the entire holiday program of The Salvation Army. They also provide a portion of the money needed to supply year-round social services for the unfortunate.

Christmas kettle funds enable the Army to provide holiday dinners for more than 500,000 families each year. And The Salvation Army plays Santa to an equal number of youngsters, making sure they are not disappointed on Christmas morning. Other activities include children's parties, hospital visitation and prison ministry. Not an age group is forgotten, from tots in orphanages to lonely people in homes for the aged.

In many cities the Salvation Army Christmas effort has become a community project. Service club members frequently man the Army's kettles for a period during the Christmas season, and it is a slippery passer-by who gets past without digging into his pocket for a donation. Other groups such as city firemen and policemen also help out.

Sometimes Christmas kettles are supplemented by special efforts like the "Tree of Lights." A mammoth tree is erected in a central location, and townspeople "buy" the privilege of turning on a Christmas tree light by contributing a certain sum of money.

Though the kettle custom is most widespread in the United States, it has caught on with success in other lands.

It was first introduced to Japan in 1906, a year of famine and unemployment following the Russo-Japanese War. The late, renowned Commissioner Gunpei Yamamuro had already been busy doing what he could for the hungry people. His wife was responsible for a home for children from the stricken areas. In the meantime her own baby boy came down with pneumonia and died.

The newspapers wrote about what had happened, and the Yamamuros' sacrifice moved the people to send in a large amount of money. With the money, Yamamuro distributed "comfort baskets." In the baskets were "mochi" (rice cakes—the special delicacy of the New Year), fruits, candy, Bibles and Salvation Army tracts.

The effort was so well received that the Army had to think about a new way of raising money. They adopted the Christmas kettle idea. "Christmas pot"—"charity pot" or "social pot" as it is literally translated from the Japanese—became well

known in the country. Today many Japanese calendars carry pictures of the "Christmas pot."

Christmas kettles have been on the streets of Rio de Janeiro, Brazil, since 1937. In Brazil the workers do not have to worry about frozen hands or feet, but rather they are troubled with the extreme heat, since December is their hottest month.

Kettles were first used in Belgium at Liege in 1934. Since that time they have been in use every Christmas season until December 6—St. Nicholas Day—when toys customarily are given to children. In Belgium the kettles are painted silver and are suspended from red and white tripods with a panel in the two national languages—French and Flemish.

The Finns have been accustomed to the sight of Salvation Army Christmas kettles for about fifty years. "Now Christmas really is coming," people say when the kettles come out. In the early days of this century, when the streets were not well lighted, a candle was kept burning in a lantern at every kettle.

Other lands in which the kettle has been used include Switzerland, France, Canada, Korea, the Canal Zone, Alaska, Hawaii, Cuba, the Bahamas and British Guyana. Aid to the needy at Christmas time is given in every country where the Army operates, but various means are used to collect funds, depending upon the laws and customs of the particular country.

But no matter where in the world you see the Christmas kettle, you will find the same spirit of cheerful service given in the name of Christ. The Salvationists who attend the kettles stand uncomplainingly in the slush, the cold, the heat or the rain. One kettle tender was startled to find his solo, "Adeste Fideles," had become a duet. A well-dressed man had joined him in singing the carol. Passers-by stopped in amazement at the sound of a powerful, well-trained voice booming out the majestic words. Then, just as quickly as he had come, the man shook hands with the kettle worker and disappeared in the crowd. One of the shoppers recognized him as a world-famous opera star.

At the end of the day another Salvationist found in his kettle a hundred dollar bill wrapped in a ragged piece of newspaper. On the paper were the words: "I came by this money dishonestly. Now I am sorry. Please use it to make someone happy."

War Cry back cover, 1955: artist unknown

War Cry cover, 1967, Max Ranft

Photo: Ron Toy, 1983

Christmas

Thank you for Christmas magic;
Stars, stables, shepherds, kings;
For children wrapped in wonder
And the sound of angels' wings!
Thanks for the gentle spirit
That descends at Christmas time,
And casts the miser out of men!
And makes our faces shine.

Upon our knees
Among the hay
We thank You Lord
For Christmas Day!

—Commissioner John Gowans
1983

A Small Gift of Love

Mary Ellen Holmes
1966

The whole story of the doll reads like a fairy tale spun from gossamer, for there is mystery in it and romance, light and shadow, tears and laughter.

Artwork: Chas. Horndorf

But if, in the end, you hear the song of angels and see a distant star, then you will know why it happened just the way it did, and why it should be told this Christmas season.

To begin with, no one really knew *where* the doll came from. It was just there, in its nurse's uniform, inside the door of the Salvation Army hall when the captain came back to pack Christmas baskets that bitter December day in 1918.

The war was over, but influenza was raging across the country. Captain Dunlap, who had been on volunteer duty at the hospital since early November, had begged an eight-hour leave that afternoon.

"Just long enough to get the baskets packed and delivered," she told he supervisor. "Where there is illness and unemployment there is also hunger. And there will be the children wishing for toys in the morning—and the old folks counting on the woolen socks and shawls the Home League has been knitting."

"God love you!" the supervisor said—and the words were not strange on her tongue, for she had grown accustomed to them during the weeks the captain had worked on the floor with her, sharing the living and the dying—"if I could, I'd help you myself!"

It was dusk when the captain left the hospital—that time of day when the world is cloaked in a gray mist of transition between sun and stars— and she did not really see the doll until her overshoe touched it just inside the front door in the dark little hallway leading into her office. She reached down and felt, rather than saw, the smooth china of the face, the bulky softness of the nurse's cap, and the piece of paper pinned to the stiff white of the uniform apron.

Under the light on her desk she read the words. "Please give this doll to some little girl who will love it. Her name is Florence."

The note was unsigned.

And so—in the beginning—no one really did know *where* the doll came from at all.

Ellen Johnson was just eight years old when the small gift of love which was the doll was given to her. Exactly eight, for she had been born on Christmas Day, and it may well be that the Christmas birthday had prompted Captain Dunlap to place the doll, carefully wrapped in white tissue, on top of the Johnson food basket.

Or perhaps it was just that, from the moment she picked the doll up in the darkened hallway, the captain had been thinking how excited Ellen would be over the white uniform, the starched cap, the nurse's apron. Ellen, who, at eight, already knew that she *had* to be a nurse some day. Ellen, who, still almost a baby herself, could soothe a crying infant with her touch, or bring a fever down, or calm a frightened, hurt child, or bandage a wound, or heal a broken bird wing.

It was a long climb up five flights of stairs to the tiny room-and-a-half where Ellen lived with her grandmother since her parents had been killed in a fire in a shabby tenement building across town, but to Captain Dunlap the bushel basket grew lighter with every step. There was a small chicken in the basket, and potatoes, milk and butter, some onions and carrots and a soup bone. There was a homemade fruit cake wrapped in Christmas tissue and a knitted, warm shoulder shawl for Granny Johnson. And on top of the basket, carefully covered with white tissue, there was the doll. It was as if Captain Dunlap carried a little of heaven and earth in her arms. And who knows, perhaps she did!

Ellen heard her coming, and rushed headlong down the last flight to meet her. "Merry Christmas, Captain!" she called from the landing, "Merry, merry Christmas!" At the child's insistence, Captain Dunlap released one wire handle of the basket toward her and together, carrying it between them as if it were a great treasure chest of gold, they climbed the fifth flight of stairs.

Inside the little apartment everything was spotless and shining. On a table near the window a lone branch of pine lent a sweet Christmas fragrance to a tiny Nativity scene, carefully, skillfully fashioned from magazine cutouts and matchsticks.

Captain Ann Dunlap lived to be 69, and until the day she died she never forgot the look on Ellen Johnson's face when she first saw the doll. Mostly it was the eyes, so large and luminous to start with, so filled with childlike hope and wonder. Christmas eyes, they were—and if you have ever met anyone born on Christmas Day you will know what that means.

The captain could not remember afterward what was said in the little room that late Christmas Eve. But she could remember, always, the eyes—the swift delight, the incredible joy, the great gratitude, and the sudden tears that welled like jewels and dropped like silver rain.

And in that room, in that moment of time and space, the captain knew that, somehow, Ellen Johnson *would* be a nurse because someone, with the small gift of love which was the doll, had given her a star to follow.

A dozen swift years came and went—and in them Ellen Johnson and "Florence" became something of a legend in Manhattan. It was as if God had granted to Ellen a special gift of healing. She had only to walk into a room and the sunshine came with her. She went gladly, willingly wherever there was suffering or pain or sorrow, and always when she left there was peace and calm behind her. If the patient were a child, then Florence accompanied Ellen, and often over the years the doll was left, clasped tightly in a child's arms, until a crisis passed, or a broken leg healed, or a rheumatic heart grew strong.

When finally, at 20, Ellen was able to enter nurse's training, she was already more a nurse than many nurses ever learn to be. When she was capped she stayed on in the hospital and, although she was often offered promotions, she preferred to be what she was—a floor nurse, with a special affinity for those who needed her most. Somehow the most irascible patients accepted her, the most critically ill rallied, the most unhappy found hope.

And so it was not unusual at all that Ellen should have taken a special interest in Mrs. Jonathan Brewster from the moment she entered the hospital, for Mrs. Brewster was all three problems in one—irascible, critically ill following a heart attack, and utterly (and volubly) unhappy.

During his lifetime, Mr. Brewster had donated generously to the hospital, and his will had left a bequest large enough to build a children's wing in memory of the little girl the Brewsters had lost many years before. Now, in her illness, Mrs. Brewster reverted often to the past, one moment haughtily demanding service, the next pitifully crooning a lullaby to an imaginary child she rocked endlessly in her arms. Vestiges of grace and beauty still clung to her body, but bitterness and selfishness so overshadowed her spirit that in the first week of her hospitalization she went through eight private duty nurses, dismissing all of them and finally deciding not to hire any more.

Dr. Brock, who attended her, was more than a little troubled, but even he could not persuade her to treat her nurses as if they were human beings. It was almost as if Mrs. Brewster hated nurses and deliberately wanted them to hate her.

The family physician who turned the case over to Dr. Brock had been stricken himself with a heart attack two days after admitting Mrs. Brewster. From his own hospital bed, he had given explicit instructions and a grave warning. "She's like a dowager without a dynasty," he advised. "All her life she's had her own way and, difficult though it will be, you'll have to appease her in every way you can. To antagonize or upset her in her present condition would be fatal."

There were many times, in the weeks which followed, when Dr. Brock wondered if it would not be fatal for him if he continued to "take" Mrs. Brewster. In the old days, he might have been able to talk out his frustration with his wife, but Dr. Brock had been a widower for three years, and so he worried only his own heart with the old lady he wanted so desperately to help.

Through it all, though, Ellen Johnson was a godsend. Not that Mrs. Brewster was any less harsh with Ellen than with the others. If anything, she was even more critical and demanding. But in spite of it—or perhaps because of it—Ellen quietly came more often than necessary to the room, ministering to Mrs. Brewster's needs, speaking gently, making her comfortable.

As Christmas approached, Ellen tried several times to share with Mrs. Brewster the plans and preparations being made in the hospital for the holiday. But Mrs. Brewster would have none of it. At the mention of Christmas she became sullen and melancholy and one day, when Ellen was especially happy over decorating the tree in the children's ward, Mrs. Brewster lashed out almost violently. "Christmas is stupid and senseless, and

so are all the people who believe in it," she declared, staring icily at Ellen.

"Never that, Mrs. Brewster," Ellen answered as gently as if she were placating a disobedient child. "Christmas is full of warmth and wisdom. The very thought of the birth of the Christ Child makes me glad inside."

"Humbug!" Mrs. Brewster snorted, and if she had learned the word from Scrooge himself she could not have delivered it more convincingly. "If there is a God He would know better than to try to save the world with a baby."

"It was the only way He could," Ellen said. "If Jesus had come to earth as a king, people might have followed Him because of His power, or His wealth. When God sent Him as a tiny baby lying in a manger He knew that people would come to Him only because they loved Him. That's what Christmas really is, Mrs. Brewster—a small gift of love to lead men back to God."

"Love!" Mrs. Brewster rejoined. "Was it love that took away my only child?"

"Love gave her to you in the beginning," Ellen said softly, "and death does not really take away, except for just a little while."

They did not speak again of Christmas until Sunday afternoon, and then it was Dr. Brock who was responsible for the incident.

Sunday was Ellen's usual day off, but she had stopped by the hospital anyway to see how Mrs. Brewster was. And so she was there, in the room, when Dr. Brock brought the Christmas tree.

It was a small artificial tree on a tiny standard, gaily decorated with old-fashioned ornaments and golden tinsel. He placed it carefully on the bedside table and smiled at Ellen across the glimmering star crowning the top branch.

"Merry Christmas to both of you," he said gaily. "I haven't had a Christmas tree since my wife died, and I decided I wanted to share it with my favorite patient."

"Get it out of here!"

The words were sharp, hysterical. "Get it out of here, I said." Mrs. Brewster raised up from the pillow, her face flushed, her mouth distorted, her breathing harsh and irregular.

In a moment Ellen had lifted the tree from the table, carried it into the corridor and rushed back to help Dr. Brock with his patient. It took a long time to calm Mrs. Brewster but finally, when she had dropped into an easy sleep, Ellen followed the doctor into the hall. He stood there awkwardly, holding the tree, looking like a small boy who had been punished for something he could not understand.

"She doesn't really mean to be unkind," Ellen said. "It's just that she's old and lonely and afraid."

The doctor looked at Ellen, her beginning-to-gray hair under the little hat reaching almost but not quite to his shoulder, and before the gentle understanding in her eyes he was suddenly ashamed and shy.

"You're right," he said. "She really is!" Then, mostly because he wanted to express the warm glow he felt stirring within him at that moment, he handed Ellen the tree. "The tree isn't much," he said, "but the ornaments were mine when I was small, and the star is one my father made."

Love comes in many different ways, but never more simply or never more beautifully than it came that Sunday before Christmas to Ellen Johnson and Dr. David Brock, standing in the hospital corridor outside the door of an irascible old woman who had been their Cupid.

The days following that Sunday were filled with work and wonder. Ellen was more nurse than ever now, for love lent a new magic to her touch; and her happiness was a golden cup, full and running over, to be shared by all her patients.

All, that is, except Mrs. Brewster who grew daily more irritable and hard to please. She was sitting up a little bit at a time now, berating everyone in the hospital, especially Ellen. But when the supervisor sent Ellen to the other end of the hallway on emergency duty, Mrs. Brewster demanded her back immediately. "She's the only one around here I can stand to look at," she said.

Finally, Christmas Eve came.

In the rest of the hospital there was the same hustle and bustle which accompanies Christmas anywhere. In the kitchen the turkeys were ready for their special stuffing; in the wards the Christmas trees were trimmed; from the hospital windows candles sent gleams across the snow; and in the corridors the carolers sang of a silent night, of a manger in Bethlehem, and of three kings bearing gifts and following a star.

But Mrs. Brewster would have none of it at all.

She asked the night nurse to close the transom, and when the carolers stopped at her door to wish her a merry Christmas she ordered them imperiously away.

She was sitting up in bed when Ellen knocked softly at the door and entered carrying the tissue-wrapped package. It was late, for there had been —as there always are—many Christmas Eve emergencies. Ellen was tired, and the tiredness showed in her eyes, but she had felt compelled all day to do what now she did.

"Merry Christmas, Mrs. Brewster," she said brightly. "I've brought you a gift."

"I have no need for gifts!"

Sullenly, Mrs. Brewster turned her face away from Ellen's look of compassion. "Merry Christmas, indeed. To me, this is only the day my daughter died." And then, as if she needed to be superior to cover up the tremor in her voice, she added icily, "What gift could you possibly give to me that would be of any value?"

"It's the greatest gift I have to give," Ellen said simply, "and I don't really know why I want you to have it, but I do."

Awkwardly she placed the box on the bed and started for the door.

"Wait!" The word was sharp, demanding, and Ellen answered the command as naturally as she would have obeyed a doctor's order. "Take the gift with you," Mrs. Brewster said, "I don't need it."

"Oh, but you do!" And suddenly all the things Ellen had wanted to say for so long were pouring out in a torrent of words—kind words, beautiful words, touched with tenderness and tolerance.

"It's more than a gift I bring you in the box," Ellen said. "It's all the things that gift meant to me. I was eight years old when someone sent it to me for Christmas. My parents were dead, and I was sometimes hungry, and always poor, and often afraid. But somehow, after that Christmas I was never really any of those things again. It was as if this were more than a gift—it was a symbol. Someone had shared love with me and kindness. Someone had sent hope to me wrapped in white tissue paper. Someone had given me a star in the darkness of my despair."

"And now ..." the whispered words came strangely from Mrs. Brewster's lips, "... and now I am poor and hungry and afraid. And all my money cannot bring me love or hope—and nowhere in the darkness can I see a star—"

"The star is there," Ellen said, "and if only you will let us, David and I will love you. That's why I brought the gift to you, to tell you now—as it told me then—that you are not forgotten."

Carefully she unwrapped the tissue from the box and placed the doll in its white uniform in Mrs. Brewster's cradled, empty arms.

For a long moment there was silence in the room, and then suddenly Ellen saw in Mrs. Brewster's eyes the same unforgettable things Captain Dunlap had seen in hers so many years before—the swift delight, the incredible joy, the great gratitude, and the sudden tears welling like jewels and dropping like silver rain.

Even before she heard the words Ellen knew—it was as if she had known from the first moment Mrs. Brewster entered the hospital.

"It's Florence!" Mrs. Brewster said slowly, unbelievingly. "It's the Christmas doll I bought so many years ago for my little girl. It's the doll I took to the Salvation Army hall the afternoon my daughter died in the flu epidemic in 1918."

And so, in the end—as it was in the beginning—the story of the doll reads like a fairy tale woven from gossamer. There is mystery in it and romance, light and shadow, tears and laughter.

But most important of all, there is in it, and running through it, the great glorious message of Christmas itself—that no kindness is ever lost, and that a small gift of love is still the world's greatest miracle.

Expectation and Realization

General Wilfred Kitching
1960

Of all the festivals in the Christian year, surely there can be none more eagerly awaited than Christmas. Its preparation takes time, and to a child it must seem that the day of all days never is going to come! The reasons that promote this spirit of expectation may be varied, but they lead up to a day in which much that has been anticipated is realized at last.

The tone and temper of many Old Testament prophets show that they had been trained to look forward to the coming of One "long expected." These men lived in a world of expectation and allowed neither delay nor discouragement to dim their hopes. "We are waiting for Him," they said; and though they died with hopes unfulfilled, there came a day when shepherds who kept "watch over their flock by night" and wise men who had "seen His star in the East" and two of God's choice servants, Simeon and Anna, witnessed the realization of the age-long vision. Expectation had not been in vain. Realization was the reward of faith.

The word of Isaiah was now fulfilled: "This is our God; we have waited for Him, and He will save us."

"This is our God!" The Babe in the crib is the manifestation of God, not far away in a heaven of music and rapture, but God on earth—where children cry in their cradles, where men tramp wearily through vales of sorrow, where homes are blighted, where fall the tears of the mourner—here on an earth scarred by the ravages of sin.

It has been rightly suggested that a religion which proclaims that God, as man, was first seen in a cradle, surely should train us in the habit of expecting Him to break into every one of life's trying situations. It is the universal witness of Christians that again and again they have seen their expectations of deliverance fulfilled in glorious reality; help has come—and freedom. "This is our God ... He will save us."

There is no one, however humble, who does not experience, in the ordinary material relationships of every day, the ebb and flow of expectation and realization as regularly as the movement of the tides. How much richer we should be if we experienced that same alternation of expectation and realization on the spiritual level. What gain would come to us if we sought, in the daily routine, some spiritual lesson interpreting in terms of the soul the commonplace experience of each day.

Jesus looked at a candle and said, in effect, "The spiritual man is a light shining in the darkness of materialism." He looked at a vine and taught that the spiritually minded man is a plant from which other men can pluck the thirst-quenching grapes of understanding. When He broke bread He made men feel that the spiritual man is to the world as bread is to the hungry.

"When you go through a door," He said, if not in so many words, "and take your rest in the cool quietness of your home, think of Me, through whom you can find rest for your soul. When you wash, think of My truth and of its cleansing power." When He invited men to look at flowers, it was to show them that God delights to express

Himself through beauty. The very cattle straining under the yoke served to illustrate His secret, which made the burdens of life easy to bear.

Jesus came to people who, though not without some expectation that the Deliverer would come, lived lives that had little meaning. He sought to show them that the real meaning of life is spiritual, that it is possible to interpret every common act of daily existence as an act of spiritual significance.

Accepting cheerfully the conditions of our environment, we can work out God's will for us in daily happenings and events. We should expect Him to break into all our actions with His presence and power, to bring us the joy of His coming. In that coming He does indeed save us, lifting us above our impotent regrets and the tyranny of our habits and evil ways. Christianity is not a spent and exhausted force; its power of influence has not come to an end. Christ constantly is breaking into the affairs of men. He does so through the dedicated lives of His followers, who, in spite of great opposition, are seeking to correct the many evils that besmirch our civilization.

However men may think of the coming of Jesus —His breaking into the life of this world— or however they may interpret His words, not one of them thinks that a more wonderful person than Christ ever will stand on earthly shores or that more beautiful and fragrant words will fall from human lips than already have fallen from His.

All the books that have been written about Him may be destroyed; the claims that devoted men and women have made for Him may be denied; men may cease to believe in the great miracles of His birth, His life and even His death and resurrection; yet will He still continue to "break into life." Wherever there are expectations about Him, realization of His presence will follow.

The existence of pain, cruelty or injustice—above all, the existence of sin—gives the thinking man a feeling that somewhere a power greater than these evils must be found. And the experience of countless people of every age and race has been that the power has manifested itself when God has "broken through" in Christ Jesus. The expectation has not been in vain!

Will you this Christmas season let Jesus "break in" upon your life? Will you let Him become real to you? If you will, the validity of His teaching suddenly will grip you. In the acceptance of that teaching and of the Savior's redemptive work, there is life. Loving God with all your heart and soul, looking on life as a spiritual reality, even though for the moment it wears the garment of the material, you will come to a condition of happy security in which great expectations are crowned with greater realizations.

Waking with the dawn, lying down at night and in all the hours between, let your prayer be that of the poet who wrote:

> *Come, Thou long-expected Jesus,*
> *Born to set the people free;*
> *From our fears and sins release us;*
> *Let us find our rest in Thee.*

Go Tell it on the Mountain

Brigadier Ivy Waterworth
1959

> *Go tell it on the mountain,*
> *Over the hills and everywhere,*
> *Go tell it on the mountain*
> *That Jesus Christ is born!*

One has only to spend Christmas at The Salvation Army's mountain missions in the hills of North Carolina to appreciate the lilting lyrics of the old spiritual. They tell precisely what Salvationists in the mountain circle are doing at this time of year.

Christmas is indeed a busy season at the Maple Springs Mountain Headquarters, where Sr.-Captain and Mrs. James Henry and their Salvationist co-workers are shoulder-deep in preparations for the Christmas cheer program.

Take the trading post, for instance. On the exterior it looks like it does at any other season, except for the wreath of galax hanging from a window and the sparkle of frost on the bearskins nailed to the front of the building. But lift the latch and step into the "supply house" of the center, and Christmas will engulf you.

Here is Santa's workshop, so full of delightful surprises that one can almost see the fat old saint bustling about among the packing boxes, knock-

26

ing over a stack of brightly dressed dolls or spilling a carton of multicolored candies across the floor for the workers to crunch under foot.

The air is heavy with mingling of delightful smells. The pungent tang of oranges, the mellow aroma of juicy, red apples, the toasty goodness of freshly roasted nuts and the tantalizing sweetness of assorted chocolates and old-fashioned candies make the place a mount of temptation to inquisitive boys and girls.

However, no one but the Salvation Army Santa and his helpers is allowed above the ground floor, for it is upstairs in the big storerooms that the mysterious surprises of Christmas are hidden. And it is there, on long tables spread with gay wrapping paper, shiny greeting stickers and rolls of colored ribbon, that the gift packages are tied.

Christmas dinners, with a fat hen and all the trimmings, are packed into baskets. Fruit, nuts and candy are added, as well as an appropriate gift for each member of the family. A store-bought cane for Uncle Doke, crippled with "arthuritis," a doll for Ruby Nell and a "kiverlet" for Granny Suttles may head the list.

The week before Christmas the mountains ring with laughter as Salvationists, in Jeeps or station wagons, take the rutted roads and hairpin curves to Boomer Den and B'ar Waller Gap, across Fairy Branch, down Hurricane Creek and up Max Patch Mountain.

Today's facile Jeep is a far cry from the old model automobile that snorted up the slopes a quarter of a century ago. The Jeeps are equipped with two-way radio, so that a girl lieutenant driving down Meadow Fork Gap may keep in touch with the captain back at Maple Springs Headquarters.

The captain smiles to himself, remembering his first winter in the mountains, then shudders at the thought of the girl lieutenant's Jeep stalled at night on a rain-swept hill. City folks could never imagine how far it is to a house—and how much farther to a telephone. They couldn't picture young lieutenants driving their Jeeps off into the night.

"The only street light in these mountains is God's moon and the stars on a clear night," he says, chuckling.

If a star shines brighter on Christmas Eve than at any other time, it is because a Salvation Army mountain lass was moved to start this ministry in honor of the Lord Christ's coming among men.

A generation has grown up since that Christmas twenty-four years ago when Captain Cecil Brown started out on horseback with her lieutenant and a young mountain lad to deliver the first holiday cheer to destitute families. That was in the heart of the depression, when even a well-to-do farmer had all he could do to make ends meet. And the hill farmers were not well-to-do.

Christmas to most of them was a day like all other days. There were few who could read the Nativity story from the old family Bible. Money was too hard come by for such foolishness as could be bought in the stores in Waynesville and Hot Springs and Canton.

The more enterprising woman would start early to put by the best of her home-canned preserves and jellies, her pickled beans and sauerkraut and hog meat. And somehow there'd be the "makings" for a pie or cake for the Christmas meal. The men and boys could bring in rabbits and other wild game.

If anyone cared to gather them, there were always mountain ivy and galax, laurel and pine cones with which to decorate the cabin. A hickory fire burning on the old stone hearth, casting its cheery light on the bare floor boards, and perhaps a "Christmas bush" on the mantel were often the sum total of cheer.

Even today the old-timers cling to their Christmas bush—a branch of balsam festooned with oversized crepe-paper flowers, with red and yellow and white and blue and pink on one bough.

But store-bought "play-pretties" for the children were out of the question. A girl child was lucky to have a doll made of wood or rags or corn husks. A boy might expect a whittled toy or, if he were most fortunate, a knife with which to whittle his own playthings.

Santa Claus and Christmas trees were practically unheard of, and when, in 1935, Captain Cecil Brown introduced her Christmas parties, the children ran from Santa. But The Salvation Army changed all that, and what began in a small way has grown into a week-long celebration in which many mountain communities have a part.

The Salvation Army lady Santa began her goodwill trek on foot and on horseback. Later she made the rounds in an old-model automobile, when roads were passable. But roads then were nothing like they are now, after years of bargaining with the state highway department to improve them.

In the mid 1940s a Jeep lightened the load of the intrepid Cecil Brown. The Jeep could climb a steep bank or splash its way through a swelling creek at the driver's slightest whim and hairpin curves and mud ruts were its delight.

One particularly mild winter a truck was used to carry Christmas over the hills. With a decorated tree firmly secured on the back, Santa, Major Brown and her lieutenants drove from settlement to settlement, holding their Christmas program out-of-doors, telling the ever-new story of the birth of the Savior.

Some of the communities boasted half-a-dozen houses within a stone's throw of each other. But only the uninitiated would be dismayed when The Salvation Army women pulled to a stop under a clump of trees in an open meadow with no sign of habitation about. Soon boys and girls would come from all directions, and following close behind were their adult kinsfolk.

"We had nary a meetin' house, but it didn't stop Christmas a'comin'," one dear old granny recalled.

At another place the truck came to a halt along a creek bank where a crowd of excited youngsters waited to offer their Christmas minstrel, pat their feet to the "banjer-pickin'" of old Doc and, reading from shaped notes (a triangle for fa, an oval for sol, a square for la, a diamond for mi), intone their favorite Christmas song, "Beautiful Star of Bethlehem."

One year the captain took down with the flu in the midst of the holiday rush, and Big Bend on the Pigeon River had to delay its Christmas until January 11. Of that visit Captain Brown wrote: "We loaded the Jeep with all our Christmas things and took off early in the morning. At the mouth of Cold Springs Creek we parked the Jeep—the road ended there—and took a sack of toys and so forth across our shoulders and started down the river to where the families live.

"When we finally came to the crossing, the water was over most of the rocks and it was impossible to get across—that is, with dry feet.

"Finally, when every suggestion as to how we would get across failed, I said, 'I'm not carrying these things back. Those children have waited long enough for their Christmas, and there is just one thing to do.'"

By that time she had her shoes and hose off and was wading across.

Many things have changed since Captain Cecil Brown first took Christmas to her mountain people, but the Salvation Army officers who serve the district today know that hard work, long hours of rugged driving, loving the people and being loved by them, preaching the redemptive power of Jesus Christ and praying many a weary sinner into the Kingdom have not changed.

With an unchanging devotion to Him who left the splendor of Heaven to dwell with men, they follow the injunction of the spiritual:

Go tell it on the mountain
That Jesus Christ is born!

Love Came Down at Christmas

John Parris
1992

LITTLE CREEK, NC—The man they call the Shepherd of the Hills spent a couple of days last week taking what he calls "Christmas cheer" to folks of the far off, lonely reaches of the Newfound Mountains of Haywood and Madison counties. In one day alone, from dawn to dusk, Brigadier James P. Henry (R) of the Little Creek Mission of The Salvation Army covered 180 miles of narrow, winding, twisting dirt roads to deliver food baskets.

"Most of these people," he said, "wouldn't have anything like a traditional Christmas dinner if it weren't for this."

His journey of Christmas cheer took him into hidden valleys and into the high coves and hollows where old ways and old customs still prevail, where the water supply still comes from a spring out back of the house, where the ax and the chopping block, the woodshed and the woodpile feed the fireplace and woodburning cookstove.

The last time Jim Henry had made such a journey was 30 years ago, when he headed up the Maple Springs Mission located in Max Patch. Then a few months later he moved on to Atlanta and assignments that took him all over the world, retiring in 1981.

His retirement brought him and his wife Ruth back to the mountains and the people they love. And when he learned that the people of this section had been without a church for 13 years, he asked Salvation Army leaders to let them reopen the Little Creek Mission, which they did last year.

And now, on this December day six days before Christmas, he again was traveling the little known backroads to bring Christmas cheer to lonely widows and others who have a hard time eking out a living in a harsh region. As he drove along in a four-wheel drive station wagon jammed with bags of food, he talked of his love for the mountains and the mountain people he serves.

"What you and I have been doing today," the 75-year-old Shepherd of the Hills said, "is what Christmas means.

"Love came down at Christmas. And there are some things you can do about Christmas. You can ignore it, or you can deplore it, or you can explore it.

"And when you explore it," he said, "you learn the meaning of Christmas. Love came down at Christmas and touched the hearts of people."

His Christmas mission took us to places few folks have ever heard of and even fewer have ever been: Bend of the River, Harmon Den, Cold Springs, Little Creek Gap, Max Patch, Lemon Gap, Long Branch, Little Creek, Meadow Fork, The Bluff and Spring Creek.

And to each of the homes where he stopped he delivered Christmas cheer that included things needed for a substantial meal for a family.

"There's a fat hen," he said, "bread in the form of rolls, all kinds of canned vegetables—corn, beans, tomatoes, pinto beans—rice, potatoes, corn meal, flour, all kinds of canned fruit and canned meat. It's a marvelous meal. Enough for several meals. And there are apples and oranges and nuts and candy, the whole works."

Jim Henry paused. When he spoke again, there was a tear in his voice. "Most homes we visit have some kind of small Christmas decoration such as a green ribbon with a ribbon bow tied about the curtains. People here can't afford Christmas trees. They can't afford the things needed to decorate them. And for the old ones it's too much to go out and cut a Christmas tree, bring it in, and even use simple, homemade decorations such as strings of popcorn and paper flowers."

We roll down into the valley and through Trust and Luck and through Betsy's Gap and back into Haywood County and to Shelton Laurel, where Jim and Ruth Henry have the home they built when they came back to the mountains.

"I've got to go out with another load of Christmas cheer tomorrow," he said. "I'll be going back to all the places we missed today. And I'll be going back before Christmas Eve to those who have little children and give toys to those who don't have any."

Jim Henry paused, nodding his head, then smiled.

"Yes," he said, "what we've been doing today is what Christmas means."

Originally reprinted from the December 22, 1991 Asheville (N.C.) Citizen Times. Reprinted here with permission of the publisher.

The Spirit of True Brotherhood

(an excerpt)
J.C. Penney
1955

What constitutes the spirit of true brotherhood? Let us consider a few of the ways in which we can apply this quality of mind to improve ourselves and the world around us.

In order so to love our fellow beings, we must exercise certain qualities of character, the most important being unselfishness. Christ said, "It is more blessed to give than to receive."

I know from my own experience that this is true, and I have found it to be so materially as well as spiritually. Having been in business now for more than 50 years, I have acquired much evidence that it can pay big dividends to be unselfish. And it has far-reaching benefits from the spiritual standpoint, too.

It is not an easy thing to develop a feeling of

love for *all* people, and yet that is what is called for by the true brotherhood spirit. If we fail to find or appreciate in some of those we encounter the good which is in everyone (and, of course, it exists in varying forms and amounts in different persons), then we are prone to dislike or fear those individuals.

We do not have the right spirit, either, if we say, "I love all men—except those who do not believe as I do." Neither are we acting right if we think: "I love all men—but I do draw the line against those whom I consider evil." If we pass such judgment on others, we have not yet learned to love fully, and here is the crux of the problem.

Many people remain too conscious of those things which make people different from one another—such things as geographical location, race, color, language, nationality, customs and creeds. In saying this, I do not mean to belittle the importance of these differences.

What I want to emphasize is the importance of looking among the fundamental issues for those points of similarity and agreement. When we find them, we then have a firm basis for understanding, friendship and cooperative effort toward a goal which is mutually desirable and beneficial.

A major component of the spirit of true brotherhood is the following through of love's motivation by applying the Golden Rule in all of our human relationships.

Christ said it thus: "Whatsoever ye would that men should do to you, do ye even so to them."

This universal rule of conduct is sound from the practical, as well as the idealistic, standpoint. I can show you prominent proof of this from my own personal experience. The department store chain which bears my name was founded by me 53 years ago in the small mining town of Kemmerer, Wyoming. My associates and I, from the start, sincerely tried to apply the Golden Rule as our basic operating principle. Our first few stores were even called Golden Rule stores. When businessmen said that our aim was impractical, they added that we wouldn't succeed in the competitive field of retailing.

Actually, our success has exceeded our most daring hopes. For years now, the Penney Company has been the world's largest department store chain.

We have seen how the spirit of true brotherhood can be considered as having three major constituents: love for one's fellows, the seeking of fundamental ties and the application of the Golden Rule.

May God, the Father of *all* mankind, give each of us the inspiration and guidance provided by a clear vision of His purpose, and may He help us to realize the love He holds for us all, and the love we should hold for each other.

Christmas Rediscovered

Brigadier Lillian Hansen
1957

Did you know that the observance of Christmas once was prohibited by law and considered a penal offense? And this, not in some faraway country, but in our own America!

Did you know that until 1856, for instance, December 25 was a common workday in Boston and that those who refused to go to work on Christmas Day often were dismissed?

Or that as late as 1870 classes were held in the public schools of Boston on Christmas Day and that any pupil who stayed at home to celebrate was severely punished?

In the early days of Christianity there was another time when the celebration of Christmas was discouraged.

Christmas originally was celebrated during a festival of the winter solstice. At this season of the year it was customary to hold great feasts in honor of heathen gods. But the early leaders of the Christian Church prohibited these primitive festivities as unsuited to the character of Christ.

Then, too, as one writer has pointed out, "The early Christians could not very well have had a Christmas in their homes when their religion was illegal and they were forced to hide in the catacombs."

Although during the first three centuries of the Christian era there was considerable opposition in the Church to "the pagan custom of celebrating birthdays," there is some indication that a purely religious commemoration of the birth of Christ was included in the Feast of the Epiphany on January 6.

Clement of Alexandria mentions the existence of the feast in Egypt about the year 200 A.D., and there is evidence that it was observed on various dates in scattered areas.

After the triumph of Constantine, and soon after the end of the last great persecution of the Christians, about the year 320 A.D., the Christians at Rome assigned December 25 as the date for the celebration of the birth of Christ. For a while many Eastern churches continued to keep other dates, but toward the end of the fourth century the Roman custom became almost universal.

The Church did not claim that we know the precise date of Christ's birth, but merely assigned a specific day in order to unify this important celebration. The fact that December 25 was chosen does not seem to rest so much on historical findings as it does on the desire to replace the popular pagan celebration of the winter solstice with the festivities of a truly Christian holiday.

On December 25 the Romans celebrated the Mithraic feast of the sun god in what they called the "Birthday of the Unconquered Sun." The Romans calculated that December 25 was the day when the sun was at its lowest ebb—ready to increase again and impart its strength to the growing things on the earth. Hence, the Roman Saturnalia, named after the ancient god of seedtime, was a boisterous holiday indeed. To the pagans, Saturnalia was fun. To the Christians, it was an abomination of homage to a disreputable pagan god.

The Christians were dedicated to the slow, uphill task of converting the pagan Romans. There were many newcomers into the ranks of Christianity, but the church fathers discovered that they also were facing an invasion of pagan customs. The habit of celebrating Saturnalia was too strong to be left behind. At first the Church forbade it, but in vain; so they tried to tame it by pointing the festival toward the Christian Sun of Righteousness.

One historian has pointed out, "It would be shallow to conclude that this was all merely a clever trick. For the most important thing that ever happened to the world was the coming of Christ, His death, His resurrection. They celebrated the event during that long interval between the dying of the old year and the birth of the new. The time of Christ's coming—according to the time the churchmen set—did fall in the midst of Saturnalia. The birthday of Christ ran the danger of being swallowed up in pagan merrymaking. The church fathers tried strenuously to keep Christmas strictly a churchly celebration. It was part of their unremitting struggle to break the grip of the pagan gods upon the people. And they broke the grip—after a battle of centuries."

In Northern Europe, as well as Rome, the winter solstice was celebrated, and the Teutonic tribes had developed many customs and traditions that became a part of the feast of Christmas when the people were converted to Christianity.

Thus, it is certain that some of the popular features and symbols of our Christmas celebration had their origin in pre-Christian yuletide customs. But Christmas itself—the feast, its meaning, its message—is in no way connected with any pagan mythology or yule rite.

Christmas became a feast of such religious importance that from the fifth century to the tenth century it marked the beginning of the ecclesiastical year.

By the early Middle Ages, Christmas had become the greatest of popular festivals. Beggar and king observed the day. Churches were decorated, and quaint plays concerning the Nativity were enacted. Carols were sung in the streets, and images of the virgin and Christ were carried from home to home. Of course there was feasting, as there always is at festival times.

The Reformation, and the subsequent suppression of the Mass, undoubtedly can be considered the immediate cause of the swing of the pendulum of law and custom away from the observance of Christmas in many countries.

In Scotland the celebration of Christmas was forbidden as early as 1583, and punishment was inflicted on all who observed it.

In England the observance of Christmas was forbidden during the Puritan ascendancy. The Puritans condemned even the religious celebration held in the Anglican Church. Indeed, they seemed determined to abolish Christmas altogether. It was their belief, apparently, that no feast of human institution should outrank the Sabbath, and because Christmas was the most important of the non Sunday festivals, they denounced its observance as sinful.

From 1642 to 1652 the Puritans in England issued a series of ordinances forbidding all church services and festivities. In 1644 a law was passed making Christmas a market day and forbidding the making of plum puddings and mince pies as a heathen custom. Parliament ruled, on June 3, 1647, that the Feast of Christmas should no longer be observed under pain of punishment. On December 24, 1652, an act of Parliament again reminded the public that no "observance shall be had on the five and twentieth of December, commonly called Christmas Day; nor any solemnity used or exercised in churches in respect thereof."

Each year, by order of Parliament, the town criers went through the streets a day or two before Christmas reminding the people that "Christmas Day and all other superstitious festivals" should not be observed and that the stores should remain open.

In America, the General Court of Massachusetts passed a law in 1659 making the observance of Christmas a penal offense. The Pilgrims, of course, worked as usual on their first Christmas Day in America, although they observed strict Sabbath rest on the preceding day, Sunday.

The observance of the Christmas holiday returned to England with the restoration of the monarchy in 1660. But over in America the zeal against Christmas persisted far into the nineteenth century. And in New England, Christmas was outlawed until the second half of the last century.

It was not until the wave of Irish and German immigration in the mid 1800s that Christmas in America really began to flourish.

The Germans brought their beloved Christmas trees, and the Irish brought the ancient custom of putting lights in the windows. Both groups brought the crib, carols and hymns, the customs of attending religious services and abstaining from work on Christmas Day. Eventually a powerful surge of enthusiasm from peoples of all countries and faiths in America swept away resistance to the celebration of Christmas.

One by one the best of the old traditions were lovingly revived.

When Christmas was rediscovered, and restored in 1660 in England, some of the fine old traditions of religious observance disappeared in large measure from the commemoration, according to some historians.

"What was left," said one observer, "was a worldly, shallow feast of amusements and reveling."

In proof, there is offered the Christmas song in praise of "plum pudding, goose, capon, mince pie and roast beef," found in *Poor Robin's Almanack* for 1695, and two descriptions of "this new kind of Christmas without Christ" found in Charles Dickens' *Christmas Stories* and Washington Irving's *Sketch Book.*

Another writer states, "After the Restoration the old observances came back—somewhat subdued—but gay and festive as ever."

Today Christians may well rejoice that throughout the world the commemoration of Christmas was rediscovered for it seems fitting indeed that the Advent should be thus remembered.

It is true, of course, that in our day materialism, self-seeking and the pursuit of pleasure are far too rampant. Even Christmas seems unable to escape some of the dangers of commercialism. But the core of the Christmas celebration is still the birthday of the Christ Child, the Son of God, the Savior of Mankind.

Christmas is a time of far more than good will—important though that is. It is a season of far more than peace on earth—desirable though that would be. Christmas is the birthday of Jesus, God's only Son, whose birth, life, death and resurrection brought the gift of salvation to all the world.

Have you accepted God's gift of salvation? Has your heart been cleansed from the guilt of sin? Are you reconciled with God, your Heavenly Father? Are you striving to please Him daily?

If not, it is important that you right now reevaluate your own life, that you search your soul, that you accept God's truth. It is only as you look beyond the superficial celebration of Christmas—as lovely, exciting and rewarding as it may be—that you can know the exquisite joy of God's smile, and that, for you, Christmas truly will be rediscovered.

One of Us

Lesa Davis
1992

No one noticed that the captain had slipped out of the room to answer a phone call. But everyone was aware of his return.

"It's a boy!" he announced with a jubilant mixture of awe and fear. Then he added the punchline. "Someone call my wife and tell her I'll meet her out front. We have to go pick up our baby!"

It wasn't quite as crazy as it sounded. They had been waiting for years to have a baby. It seemed it would never happen. Until the phone call came. Then a baby was waiting for them.

A few hours later, they returned with a tiny pastel-wrapped bundle. Inside, held tenderly and a little awkwardly, lay a bald, beautiful little boy. Everyone oohed and cooed and softly reached out to touch his chubby little baby hands. It was, as life's greatest moments tend to be, a little bit breathtaking and speech-defying. Then the proud new father broke the silence. "Everyone," he said, "this is our son."

What more could he say? An anonymous infant had become a member of the family. Not one of "them," but one of us. Not a statistic, but a son.

Christmas celebrates the birth of another Son. "It's a boy! Just like God promised," rang out of the stable in Bethlehem. Another adoptive father looked on with wonder at someone else's Son. On that event, the coming of Christ into the world, hangs all of human history.

Writing about the overwhelming impact of that birth, the Apostle Paul explained, "When the time had fully come, God sent His Son, born of a woman, born under law, to redeem those under law, that we might receive the full rights of sons" (Galatians 4:4-5, NIV).

Jesus, fully divine, became fully human. He entered our world through the mysterious process of human birth. The pre-existent, eternal Son of God toddled from childhood through awkward adolescence to manhood in a real place with a name and a history all its own. He became a member of the human family.

If you read the Gospels, you will indeed find the miracle-working, storm-stilling Son of God. But you will also find the Son of Man. You will find that He occasionally sighed with disappointment. He got tired and hungry and needed to be alone sometimes. He knew the empty ache of a graveside, the exhilaration of a wedding reception. He felt the icy stab of betrayal, the loneliness of humiliation. Finally, He endured physical suffering and death at the hands of those who misunderstood and hated Him.

Why did He do it? "That we might receive the full rights of sons." He became the Son of Man so that the rest of us could become the children of God. In his humanity He identified Himself with our weakness. His divine power transforms and empowers us to live above it.

Without Him, we are orphans, left to ourselves in this confusing, chaotic, maddening world. He came to adopt us, to bring us home to the Father, to make us heirs of the Kingdom of God.

"To all who received him," John wrote, "to those who believed in his name, he gave the right to become children of God" (John 1:12, NIV). To all who will receive Him He still offers the right to become the children of God. At this season of celebration, will you receive Him? Will you come home to the Father?

A Candle for Barbara

Phyllis Reynolds Naylor
1980

As usual, Helen Roberts sensed, rather than saw, that Barbara Duffey was waiting for her attention. But Peter, who had put his left boot on his right foot, was prancing around the room and distracting the other children of the fourth grade from the task of putting on their own coats and galoshes.

Helen tried hard to control her impatience. She did want to keep the atmosphere cheerful even in the last turbulent two minutes before the Christmas holidays, but she was eager to get home to her own family.

Peter gave her an impish grin, kicked vigorously, and sent the boot sailing dangerously near a windowpane. The near miss had a generally sobering effect, and Helen turned toward the little girl waiting near her desk.

Barbara the barbarian, one of the more precocious children had dubbed her almost the first day she came to school. Barbara's dresses were always stained with dirt and food, her hair always matted and uncombed. Her shabby shoes, much too big for her, were obviously hand-me-downs.

Helen had wondered more than once about Fred Duffey, knowing vaguely that he cleaned stables at racetracks, moving from state to state as his work required, dragging his uncared-for and apparently unloved little daughter with him.

"What is it, Barbara?" Helen asked, trying hard not to think what the child's Christmas would be like.

"My dad sent you a note. I forgot to give it to you sooner."

Unfolding the crumpled scrap of paper, Helen read the penciled scrawl: "I will be gone two weeks and it's vacation so my girl will be by herself. Can you take her to the Children's Home after school today—it's so far to walk and she lost her boots."

"Do you know what this note says?" Helen asked.

Barbara nodded with complete unconcern.

"Have you been to the Home before?"

Barbara nodded again. "If you drop me off at the corner by the statue, I could walk the rest."

The room was empty now except for the girl and her teacher. As Barbara began to assemble her scattered crayons, Helen stood staring down at her desk. Could Fred Duffey have cunningly foreseen how she would react to his daughter's situation? Or did he actually think a teacher could callously drop his child at the Children's Home a few days before Christmas?

Then she faced the real questions. Did she dare take Barbara into the intimacy of her home for two weeks? How would her children feel about having a dirty, sullen little stranger intrude upon the happiest time of their year? What would Wallace say if she did bring

Barbara home? What would he say if she didn't?

She closed her desk drawer with a bang and gave Barbara a sudden smile. "How would you like to spend Christmas at our house?"

Barbara bent to pick up a crayon, and Helen could not see her face, but her voice was as flat as ever. "It don't make any difference. I could walk from the statue."

Helen tried again, lying valiantly. "We'd like very much to have you come, Barbara. I think you'd have a lot of fun with Susan and Mike. They're a little younger than you are, but you could have fun together anyway!"

Still stuffing broken crayons into the box, Barbara seemed only to have half-heard. "Okay," she said at last. "But you better call Mrs. Cary— that's our landlady—and tell her. The Home always does when I get there."

All the way home, Barbara sat silently with her arms clasped tightly around the paper bag with the clothing she'd brought to school that morning. A pitiful lot, Helen thought, to last a child for two weeks.

In the carport, she could hear the sound of feet thudding inside the house as Mike and Susan raced to meet her at the kitchen door. At the sight of Barbara, their mouths dropped wide, and Helen spoke quickly. "Guess what? I've brought Barbara and she's going to stay with us for two whole weeks!"

Then, as Wallace came into the kitchen with the remains of a broken ornament in the dustpan, "This is Mr. Roberts, my husband, Barbara. Barbara's father had to go out of town, Wallace, so I invited her to spend the Christmas vacation with us."

Husband looked at wife, piecing together in a flash the fragments she'd given him in the past about this pupil—the girl who didn't know how to use a handkerchief; the girl who went for a week with a broken finger before someone discovered it; the girl who squirmed uncomfortably when Helen once called her "dear."

"Well," he said slowly, "We'll really have a good time this year, won't we, kids?" Then he looked back to Helen. "It's time we did some sharing."

And share they did—doggedly, day after day. Even the children shared from the outset without too much coaching. After supper, Mike got out his checkerboard and asked Barbara to play, but she shook her head indifferently and tried to efface herself even more among the pillows on the couch.

In place of the usual bedtime story, Helen got out the portfolio of Nativity pictures she'd collected through the years, and for the first time Barbara's face took on some expression. When Helen, holding the pictures up one by one, came to "The Gift of the Magi," Barbara said with sudden decision and intensity, "I like that the best. I wish my dad could see it."

"Then take it home with you," Helen said. "I can easily get another for us." But as she handed over the picture, she could not help wondering what Fred Duffey would say when presented with it—or whether he'd say anything at all.

So the sharing went on. Wallace even took pains to work the little guest into all the family shots he took of the tree at various stages of its decoration, the hanging of the stockings on Christmas Eve, the opening of the presents on Christmas morning. And Barbara seemed to have as many packages as Susan and Mike. "Santa" had left her a new bracelet and necklace set, a jeweled hairbrush and a music box. With bright wrappings, Helen and Susan had made used clothing donated by neighbors seem almost like new gifts. Barbara, however, opened the gifts methodically and set them aside as though they did not really belong to her. Helen could only shake her head in bewilderment.

There was turkey for dinner and candymaking in the afternoon. Then, after the sun had set, the family went through a little ceremony that was uniquely theirs and which the children seemed to cherish—perhaps because Mike had first proposed it. Where he'd picked up the idea puzzled Helen, but Wallace thought their son must have seen something like it on TV. Anyway, they repeated the ritual every year.

First the lights were turned out and they stood around a table with a big red candle, each holding a small white taper. Then Mike solemnly explained to Barbara, "Dad will light the red candle and then we'll all light our little candles from the big one."

When the five small wicks were flaming, he continued, "Now here is the special thing. When you mix your fire with my fire, it means we're friends forever. Watch!" He demonstrated by merging the flame of his candle with Susan's. "Now, Barbara, you do it with me," he directed, and slowly she brought her candle to his.

Last to meld flames as the ritual continued around the circle were pupil and teacher. Helen saw that Barbara had managed to spot her new Christmas dress with hot wax—but she saw also that the child's eyes themselves were like candles in the semidarkness.

After the candle ceremony and Christmas Day, the rest of the holidays were anticlimax. Helen had planned to catch up on her reading, but spent the time altering clothes for Barbara and thinking up special things for her to do. Despite all their best efforts, Barbara seemed to be saying, "I can never be a part of you. Just let me watch."

Two days before vacation was over, the landlady called to say Barbara could come home because her father had returned. She did not say good-bye to the children or show any regret about leaving. She simply walked to the car with her greatly increased bundle of belongings and got in.

Was it worth it? Helen wondered, watching Wallace back the car down the drive. She remembered wryly the private moments she had wanted to share with Wallace when this strange little girl with observant eyes followed their every move, the times the four of them had interrupted their laughter over family jokes because they suddenly realized Barbara was left out. She was not even sure Barbara had wanted to come. Perhaps she had friends at the Children's Home. Perhaps she would have had a better time there. There was so much, Helen felt as she turned from the window, that she could never understand.

The first day back at school was typically Januaryish. Somehow Helen felt as dull and gray inside as the day itself, even though she had made a point of putting on the becoming red jersey she'd bought at one of the after Christmas clearance sales. Most of the children were wearing some new Christmas garment, and Barbara too appeared in her Christmas Day dress, with egg stains added now to the candle grease. Obviously the jeweled hairbrush had not been overused.

"It wasn't worth it," Helen whispered to herself. Nothing that had happened had any meaning to Barbara—nothing would carry over to make her life richer. She and Wallace and Mike and Susan had acted as babysitters and given the girl some warm clothing. That was the sum of it and she might as well write it off and forget it.

But the children were not ready to forget Christmas, and Helen allowed them half an hour's "telling time." To many in the class, the high point of Christmas had been decorating the tree, or the fun they'd had spending their own shopping money, or the new bike. Peter told about going to midnight mass for the first time. Esther told the class about her family's celebration of Hanukkah.

When Barbara's turn came, several moments elapsed in silence, and the girl seemed glued to her chair. Helen realized with a pang that Barbara had nothing to say. Nothing had happened that had any lasting meaning for her. As gently as possible she said, "You don't have to tell us anything, Barbara. It's up to you."

"But I do want to tell it," Barbara said. "It's just that I don't know what it's called—the thing with the candles."

"That doesn't matter," said Peter. "Tell us anyway."

Thus encouraged, Barbara slipped from her seat and moved to face the class. "Well, at our house last night we had Christmas. It's something you do with candles, but my Dad and I didn't have any candles so we used matches instead. We each struck a match and then we held them close together so the fire mixed, and then—then we were friends for life."

She looked proudly about the roomful of children, awed by her mystical little tale, and suddenly she broke into a radiant smile. "It was the very nicest Christmas I ever had in my life."

And finally, Helen understood.

Alive and Well and Living in Egypt

General Arnold Brown
1978

The angel of the Lord appeareth to Joseph in a dream, saying, Arise, and take the young child and his mother, and flee into Egypt, and be thou there until I bring thee word: for Herod will seek the young child to destroy him. When he arose, he took the young child and his mother by night, and departed into Egypt: and was there until the death of Herod: that it might be fulfilled which was spoken of the Lord by the prophet, saying, Out of Egypt have I called my son.
—Matthew 2:13-15

The incident is heavy with drama. Maniacal in his obsession to eliminate a helpless infant who he fears puts his throne at risk, a vicious king slaughters two thousand babies in history's grossest act of infanticide. Their crime? The misfortune of not having passed their second birthday.

The wanted Child escapes. A man, Joseph, has a dream. Directed by it he takes the Child and its mother, Mary, into the land of pharaohs and pyramids. Concerned relatives may eventually get word that the trio is alive and well and living in Egypt.

When the murderous king dies, man, woman and Child return to the home land. Caution, however, is still necessary. The new ruler is the dead king's son. His attitudes are unknown.

The flight into Egypt reminds us that the life of Jesus, rather than Herod's throne, was at risk from the moment of birth. Hardly had the song of the angels died away than the edict for annihilation was shouted from one military command to another.

Hardly had the brightness of the eastern star faded than the Child, lately worshiped by the wise kings, is a refugee without any star to lead to safety. Hardly had the shepherds returned to the Bethlehem plains and the minding of their sheep than He who was born to be the "Deliverer" is at the mercy of the elements and highway robbers.

The joy of the angels and the glow of the Christmas star apart—explained by the fact that Heaven knew the end from the beginning the birth of Jesus, in earthly terms, is summed up in the despairing words: "He came unto His own, and His own received Him not."

It is Egypt rather than Judea that offers shelter. It is in the land where, generations before, Joseph's forefathers had felt the lash of the whip that the Child finds asylum. As an escapee He finds protection where the race into which He was born had suffered abject slavery. The life of Jesus at its start is significantly an identification with the unemancipated; He survives where once the sting of subjection, the crushing weight of oppression, was something less than a way of life.

The name and the promise. "Emmanuel"—"God with us"—is demonstrated from the very beginning of Christ's career. He came, as someone has said, not to be "with them" but to be "with us." With us who are in bondage to sin and to ourselves; with us who need deliverance from our fears; with us for whom emancipation would mean a new chance, a new life and new hope: with us who are "across the border" from the Promised Land, joyless and futureless in the place of our ancient bitternesses.

"With us," but not passively. He will be our Emancipator, our Deliverer, our Redeemer. The real, human Baby has not ceased to be God. He has all power. He is able to lead into an eternal Canaan. As the Child of Bethlehem, Christ was no less God than before He had begun to be man. He was God plus all that He had made His own by taking manhood to Himself.

"He, who had always been God by nature," writes the Apostle Paul, "did not cling to His prerogatives as God's equal but stripped Himself of all privilege by consenting to be a slave by nature and being born as a mortal man. And, having become man, He humbled Himself by living a life of utter obedience, even to the extent of dying, and the death He died was the death of a common criminal" (Philippians 2:6-8, Phillips). And all this was for our salvation!

The sojourn in Egypt should be seriously pondered by all who, during the Christmas season, will contemplate the meaning which underlies the song of angels, the brightness of a star, the worship of shepherds and wise men, and the gladness of a Messiah's birth. This Child is the Deliverer who will march at the head of that greater exodus—"from darkness into God's most marvelous light." With Him there is no faltering or uncertainty. He is Himself "cloud by day and pillar of fire by night." Nothing can stop Him when in His sovereign saving grace, He pardons past sins, empowers the life with His own presence and guides the liberated soul into a spiritual land "flowing with milk and honey."

"With us" and "among us" are key and comforting phrases in the Christmas story. "And the Word was made flesh, and dwelt among us." The Word incarnate in human flesh is the Word incarnate in the sorrows and sufferings of man. The Baby in the manger at Bethlehem is none other than the eternal Word of God "among us."

But has this thought any meaning for today's troubled humanity? Without question! It means that Christ came with one paramount objective, that of saving man from all that binds and enslaves him, from everything that reduces life to hopelessness and makes eternity a prospect of despair. "Thou shalt call His name Jesus: for He shall save His people from their sins."

The promised Savior begins His earthly journey where His human ancestors knew their cruelest oppression, where their firstborn escaped extinction only by "the sprinkling of blood." Firstborn and only-begotten Son of God, His earthly journey ends on a cross, for "without shedding of blood is no remission." He is nailed there by those who have His nation firmly under heel.

The meaning sharpens. It is love, sacrificial love, which identifies itself with the pains and problems of men. Only love that goes "all the way" can break all chains. If a Man must die in order to fix this divine thought in the mind of mankind, then so be it. Even death is not resisted by love. Already "acquainted with grief," the Christ is willing to be acquainted with the ultimate agony. He knows—and through Him so do we—that this is the ultimate victory.

The Christmas story includes the angels' song with its matchless motif of "peace and goodwill." It includes the terror and the wonderment of the shepherds who heard it. It includes also the mystery of a guiding star and the adoration of the sages who followed it. But it also includes a monarch's persecution and a panic-stricken flight into alien territory so that prophecy may be vindicated—"That it might be fulfilled which was spoken of the Lord by the prophet, saying, 'Out of Egypt have I called my Son'."

Birth, life, death and resurrection combine in the wondrous story of Christmas. But the linking theme is unique: Emmanuel—God with us, among us, and, incredibly and marvelously, for us!

War Cry, 1996: "Flight into Egypt," Vladimir Mazuranic

To daily give of your own gifts,
To reach gladness through sorrow,
To learn sympathy through suffering,
To strengthen faith through perplexity,
To find truth through confusion,
To see the star through the mists of night:
Behold, this is good will. This is peace.
This is Christmas!
—General Evangeline Booth, 1955

War Cry cover, 1992: Karen Yee Lim

The War Cry

If God should want to speak to Man,
Say something good,
The words He chose
Would have to be
Well understood.
One single lovely Word he said,
And laid it in a manger-bed.
—Commissioner John Gowans, 1995

War Cry cover, 1953: artist unknown

War Cry cover, 1986: Ferdinand Petrie

The Crowded Inn—
A Parable of the Human Heart

Colonel Henry Gariepy
1986

"There was no room for them in the inn" are the familiar words from Luke's account of the Advent. The inspired chronicler deemed it important enough to make it a part of the record.

"No room in the inn." There is a plaintive, a poignant touch and tone to the statement. No room for the holy family who had to come to Bethlehem for the census. No room for the woman about to deliver her child.

No room for the very Son of God who had left His ivory palaces. No room for the One who had descended the steps of glory, who had divested Himself of His might and majesty to take upon Himself our humanity. No room for the Christ child.

Man offered no room for the One whose infinite splendor eclipses the paltry possessions of earth's wealthiest monarch. The One who flaunts His glory with orbiting spheres and light years had to be born in a cattleshed. An improvised feeding trough became His cradle. Lowly animals were among the first to hear the sound of God through human vocal chords. As a birthing place was sought for the Christ child, the response of man was "We have no room."

An imaginative soliloquy of the innkeeper is given by Amos R. Wells:

Could I know
That they were so important? Just the two,
No servants, just a workman sort of man,
Leading a donkey, and his wife thereon,
Drooping and pale—and I saw them not myself,
My servants must have driven them away.
But had I seen them, how was I to know?
Were inns to welcome stragglers, up and down
In all our towns from Beersheba to Dan,
Till He should come? And how were men to know?
There was a sign, they say, a heavenly light
Resplendent; but I had no time for stars.
And there were songs of angels in the air
Out on the hills; but how was I to hear
Amid the thousand clamors of an inn?

Of course, if I had known them, who they were,
And who was He that should be born that night,
For now I learn that they will make Him King,
A second David, who will ransom us
From these Philistine Romans—who but He
That feeds an army with a loaf of bread,
And if a soldier falls, He touches him
And up he leaps, uninjured? Had I known,
I would have turned the whole inn upside down,
His Honor, Marcus Lucius, and the rest,
And sent them all to stables.

So you have seen Him, stranger, and perhaps
Again may see Him? Prithee say for me
I did not know; and if He comes again,
As He surely will come, with retinue,
And banners, and an army—tell Him, my Lord,
That all my inn is His to make amends.
Alas, alas! To miss a chance like that!
This inn that might be chief among them all—
The birthplace of the Messiah—had I but known!

The crowded inn of the Christmas story is a parable of the human heart. Why was there no room for Christ at the inn? No doubt it was filled with other guests who crowded Him out. Or perhaps the innkeeper was so busy with his duties and the brisk business the census brought his way, that he had no time for other claims or needs.

Christ is still crowded from the heart and life by other claims that press upon us. We have invited other interests into our lives and have left no room for Him. Christ is not our priority.

All too often our busyness keeps us from knowing who it is that knocks at the door of our heart. We do not mean to exclude Him but the clamor and crowd preoccupy us and we miss the infinite gift of enrichment He would bring to our lives.

A song we sing in The Salvation Army probes our priorities:
Room for pleasure, room for business
But for Christ the crucified,
Not a place that He can enter
In the heart for which He died.

Room for Jesus, King of Glory!
Hasten now, His word obey!
Swing your heart's door widely open,
Bid Him enter while you may.

Let us each this Christmas have as our prayer the old Welsh Grace:

Let not our hearts be busy inns
That have no room for Thee,
But cradles of the living Christ
And His nativity.

Christmas Island

Mary Ellen Holmes
1962

If you are ever lucky enough to visit Christmas Island off the rockbound coast of Maine, the natives will point out, with pride and affection, the home of Joseph and Mary Carpenter.

It is a tight, compact, freshly painted, little white house set in the very center of the village. Every beam and rafter, every floor board has been laid carefully by the islanders themselves in recognition of their miracle—the miracle which gave Christmas Island its name.

In the neat white house, 37-year-old Joseph Carpenter, his wife, Mary, and their eight-year-old son live happily and comfortably—at peace with each other and with the world. One large front room is a sort of Yankee traders' shop, where the villagers do a land-office business swapping everything from boats to baked goods. The islanders pay the Carpenters for the space as well as for running the shop. And so, even though Joseph is a victim of Parkinson's disease, he is independent and self-supporting.

You would never guess, watching the villagers bustling in and out day after day, that there *had* been a time—not too long ago—when everyone had signed a petition to have the Carpenters evicted.

Not from this house, mind you. They were living in the lighthouse then, and that is where the story really begins. For this is the story of the lighthouse on Gull Island, the lighthouse which gave Christmas Island its name on the 25th morning of December in 1959.

To begin, Mary and Joseph Carpenter bought the lighthouse—lock, stock and barrel—for $460. It was hopelessly run-down, a derelict tower rising sharply at the sea's edge, unpainted, weather-whipped, with a ribbon of water separating it from Gull Island. But to the Carpenters, it was their ivory tower.

By trade, Joseph had been an automobile mechanic—a good one, with his own little shop in Portland. He was shocked to learn that September day three months before that he had Parkinson's disease—progressive, chronic, incurable. With their first child expected in December, they didn't know quite what to do. Joseph's limbs already were getting stiff.

Joseph's life expectancy was no doubt long, but if he were unemployable, how could he possibly plan a future for himself, for Mary, for his child? Carefully he had checked his savings, sold his shop, counted his assets. And then, almost as if it were a godsend, he had heard about Gull Island Lighthouse. By a fluke of "horse trading" it had come into the possession of a Portland merchant who was glad to sell it. For the Carpenters it was an answer to prayer—a seeming solution to all their problems. In a small place like Gull Island, the cost of living would be less than in the city. The pace would be slower. They might even find some way to supplement their savings.

And so on the tenth of November, 1959, Joseph and Mary Carpenter came to their ivory tower.

If they had guessed how violently the villagers would react to what they termed "outsiders" taking up residence in the lighthouse, they might have hesitated. But they had no way of knowing how proud and hidebound, how steeped in tradition the islanders were.

Their troubles began as soon as they reached the dock.

First, there was no boat for rent to ferry them

across the small strip of water from the island itself to the lighthouse. And finally when Joseph, in desperation, bought one, he paid $50 for an old flatbottom scow not worth ten dollars.

Supplies were next, and here, too, Joseph and Mary met the undisguised resentment of the villagers. When Mary protested that the prices marked on the shelves were much lower than the prices they had paid, the storekeeper merely grunted, "Ayeh. Not to outsiders."

From the very beginning everything went the same way. It was very clear that Gull Island wanted no part of "squatters in the lighthouse," and the sooner Joseph and Mary Carpenter headed back to the mainland, the better it would be for all concerned. Joseph *would* have gone back, too, many times. But for some strange reason, Mary would not leave. Especially, she would not leave after she found in the lighthouse storeroom the old driftwood cradle.

"Don't ask me to go now, Joseph," she pleaded. "I can't explain why; I don't know why. I only know that our baby has to be born here. Later, if you still wish it, I'll go. Oh, indeed, I'll gladly go! But not yet."

So the Carpenters stayed. November lengthened into December. Joseph's disease, aggravated by the conditions around him, grew worse. His arms trembled more, and it became harder and harder for him to make the trips to the village for supplies and kerosene—especially the kerosene, for it was heavy and awkward to handle, and he could bring only a little at a time.

It seemed to Joseph that the villagers, watching him trying to haul the five-gallon cans, were just waiting for the day when he could no longer manage them at all. It was as if they were saying, "When the kerosene is gone, they'll have to move; they'll have no heat, no light, no food."

The disease would take many years to break Joseph Carpenter's body, but what the islanders did to his spirit in six short weeks was a terrible thing. And what the entire experience did to his own soul was even worse, for gradually Joseph began to hate—the place, the people, even God Himself.

Until that Christmas morning.

There was no doctor on Gull Island. Only Joseph was with her when their son—a fine, strong, handsome manchild—was born at midnight on Christmas Eve. Only Joseph was with her to wonderingly pick up his son in his arms

and to stand straight and tall—not trembling now—looking across the strip of sea to the land where they had been refused room—and kindness—and understanding.

And then a strange thing happened to Joseph. He tried to put it into speech afterward, but there were no words. He only knew that as he held the baby in his arms, a great joy suddenly welled up within him, and he wanted to share this supreme moment of his happiness with all the world.

In that instant there was no longer any room inside him for fear of his disease or for hatred.

He turned from the bed, still holding the baby close against his chest lest his weakened hands should slip. He knew as he looked across the strip of sea to the land beyond, that nothing mattered anymore. All the frustration and bitterness were gone, as if they never had been. Here in Joseph's arms was only hope—hope eternal, hope born in his son, just as it has been born in every child since the world began.

Gently Joseph gave the baby back to Mary and watched as she laid him in the driftwood cradle. And then, because he wanted to share this moment with the people on Gull Island, because he wanted to shout out loud to them "Behold, my son. May he grow up a credit to your village." Because he wanted to say, "I'm not angry any more, nor hurt or afraid. I only want to share with you this happiest moment of my life," he took from his precious store of kerosene enough fuel to fill the five huge lamps in the lighthouse windows.

He set them blazing, like large candles in the dark, and the five beams spread out in five directions, like the points of a giant star.

Some of the islanders saw the light. A few of them even thought it might be a distress signal, but they couldn't have cared less. And, so, unconcerned, they went about their affairs.

It was six o'clock on Christmas morning before they really found out, six o'clock when the radio commentators first began to flash across the nation the story of the miracle.

How could the villagers have guessed that at exactly midnight Mary Carpenter had given birth to her firstborn son and laid him in a driftwood cradle shaped like a manger?

And how could they possibly have known that at ten minutes past twelve, just as Joseph lit the lamps to proclaim to the world that his son had been born, the pilot of a giant airliner, lost in fog off the coast with his plane's communication system jammed, suddenly had seen the heavens open up around him and a huge five pointed beacon shine through?

The pilot tried to explain later to the reporters in Portland what had happened, but, like Joseph, he could not put it into words. All he could tell was that as the sky broke into light around him, he saw, in one horrified instant, that his plane was heading straight toward a crash landing in the center of Gull Island—with its multitude of snug little homes clustered close together; Gull Island with its families sleeping, unaware of danger.

Sharply he veered his craft back into the upper channels of air and out to sea. Then, with the beacon to guide him, he found his course and,

like a wise man led by a star, carried his 88 passengers to a three-point landing in Portland, leaving Christmas Island quietly asleep under its Christmas star.

Now you know how the island got its name, and why the villagers built the house for Joseph and Mary Carpenter. You know, too, why Christmas Island seems so different from much of the rest of the world. The reason is that a spirit pervades the island—a spirit of love, understanding and tolerance that is rare, genuine and wonderful.

It is a spirit that never can die because it is part of the miracle of Christmas which, after all, began with the birth of a Baby and the star of forgiveness His Father lit to save our world.

And Dwelt Among Us

Commissioner Arthur Pitcher
1980

The phrase caught me, held me and would not let me go. It is one thing to be a tourist, catching the exotic breezes from a zephyred isle, or even a reporter, moving for a short while on the seamy side of a great city, but the Christmas story is not of a visitor, but of a resident, who shares our human condition, bears our human burdens, inhabits our human personality and identifies with us in our human dilemmas.

The relevance of Christmas came home to me as I sat in the light of a Christmas tree in a Salvation Army children's home in a Caribbean town. The costumes were traditional, the crib was homemade, the background was the living room of the home, but the characters in the drama brought a lump into my throat.

Mary was a little girl with a congenital heart disease. Pale, but glowing with the importance of her role, she sat there smiling while Joseph, an abandoned child of the city, looked protectively down on the baby. The baby had some experiences that linked her, for she was a little girl, to the first Babe of the manger. Certainly, like Him, she was despised and rejected, and certainly like Him, she had no place to lay her head. Found in an abandoned shack on the mountain side, she was brought physically depressed and frightened

to the home. But she looked so happy and comfortable there on the pillows among the straw.

Those wise men marching up the aisle were at least wise in the ways of suffering and loneliness: one had been born in the infirmary, and the other two had never known a father. The shepherds, too, were the children of broken homes and bereft lives. "Away in a manger," they sang, and as they sang, it all fell into place. "He dwelt among us."

To the abandoned and forsaken, to the child victims of a callous or uncaring society, to the sons of men committing the sins of men, He came, not to be an idle spectator or a passing stranger, but to forever be present where He is most needed.

When Peter the Great of Russia wanted to know how his laboring subjects lived, he left his throne to dwell among them. When Elisabeth Elliot wished to win the men whose spears had killed her husband, she went to live among them. Love has long ago discovered that only in involvement, only in identification, can its saving and healing ministry be manifested.

It is strangely significant that in the days when man tries to salvage something from the debris of his own destruction, when his crises of energy or international communication or economic survival loom, it should be in that era that he launches an "International Year of the Child."

Perhaps man is instinctively discovering that his only hope is in a new generation. His future lies with the child.

> *Split your atoms, cross your frontiers,*
> *Stand on yonder lunar face.*
> *Wrest its secrets from creation,*
> *Seek to build your super race.*
> *But you fail, like men of Babel*
> *Scattered, prodigal and defiled,*
> *If you find the heights of glory*
> *But in finding lose your child.*

That child, stranger of Bethlehem, in His coming, in His dwelling and eventually in His sacrificial dying, has made it forever clear that in dwelling among us, in being identified with us, He has demonstrated that He loved the lost children of men—loved them so, that for twenty centuries He has by His Spirit shared their world and involved Himself with them with divine purpose. As one cryptic sentence has put it, "The Son of God became the son of man so that the sons of men might become the sons of God."

Christmas Corridors

War Cry Staff
1973

While streets across America glisten with fairy lights and echo to the chatter of shoppers, behind the solemn facades of research centers, nursing homes, veteran's hospitals, penal and countless other institutions thousands await the holiday in lonely vigil.

Wheelchairs and stretcher trolleys ply corridors decked with Christmas trees and holiday greens. Tucked away in corner rooms, or comfortably settled in spacious lounges, are dear ones who may never again be part of the street scene.

Some are fortunate to receive visits from friends or family. Others only listen for the step that never comes and the voice that never speaks.

It is to these, especially, that the Salvation Army League of Mercy ministers with personal visits, prayers, a well-chosen Scripture reading, a home-baked treat, a fun time of games, the singing of carols and, of course, a gift for everyone.

Not all League of Mercy visitors are adults. Young people and children are often pressed into service, especially at holiday time when days off from school permit their participation.

To see 11-year-old Linda assisting Mrs. O'Leary to her room, and 12-year-old Jerry pushing the wheelchair of blind Mr. Corbett, leaves the impression that youth waits only an outlet to its capacity for compassion.

A comprehensive documentary of League of Mercy services in the United States alone would fill volumes never to be written. For wherever there is a Salvation Army of volunteer workers, there is a mind and heart awake to the peculiar situation of the moment.

Except to conform to institutional rules and regimen, there is no limit to what service may be rendered. And workers delight in going "all out" to serve the most unusual need.

Through cooperation with the Salvation Army's varied services, loved ones are reunited; the family of a prisoner receives gifts from Dad or Mom; a hospitalized veteran may select a doll for Susie or a truck for Steve.

A few stories border on the miraculous. Something in the carols sung by Salvationists struck a familiar chord in a Navy veteran who had been unable to speak for years. Staff members turned in amazement as he broke into song—the first step to recovery.

In a similar circumstance, a young worker brought her 18-month-old daughter along to the nursing home her group was visiting. The toddler worked her own charm on the residents.

One woman who would not respond to any stimulus was stirred by tiny Danielle to utter her first words.

A house of correction guard called out: "Please, Salvation Army, sing 'Away in a Manger' for me." As the group sang, one by one the men in the cells joined in, until the old building echoed to the simple children's song.

"The residents at one home called for favorite

carols. We sang, and sang, and sang, until we were hoarse, and my fingers just wouldn't play another note on the accordion," said the major in charge.

In another, mentally retarded adults (decked in bibs for lunch time) joined with delight in the fun. And the children almost lifted the roof with "Jingle Bells."

When each child was presented a pair of gaily-colored house slippers handmade by the League of Mercy, an attendant remarked: "I can count on one hand the children having a pair of slippers."

As several elderly ladies in one home sang "Stille Nacht" and "O Tannenbaum," their eyes reflected the candlelight of childhood Christ-

masses across the sea.

And at a veteran's hospital the Army band and timbrelists received a standing ovation.

Amid the joy there is often tears. Two ladies holding a sad vigil by their sister in a death coma, asked the Salvationists to sing "Silent Night."

Miraculously the song and its message reached the unconscious woman who stirred and smiled, her only sign of recognition while in the coma. The officers stayed to pray with the sisters and were there when the woman passed away.

The scenes are repeated in small or large measure wherever the league of mercy is at work. And it is the quality of love, not of talent, that moves the human heart.

Fears and Cheers

General Albert Orsborn
1951

Christmas customs differ widely in lands where the coming of the Christ Child is celebrated. They vary according to the nature of the people, and are influenced by ancient traditions and even by climatic conditions. What should be suitable amid the sparkling frost and the driven snow of the arctic would be strangely out of harmony with the shimmering heat and the arid conditions of the torrid zone.

In some lands the celebrants are within the warmth and protection of home or church; in others, they keep their Christmas in the open air under conditions which the folk in colder latitudes could envy.

Yet vary as they may in form, all the world-wide Christmas festivities have these features— the Babe of the manger is at the center of the story, and the celebrations show forth the spirit of happiness and good will. In many lands we refer to Christmas as a time of "good cheer." Many a time the carol-singers, mainly young children, at my door have called to me:

Christmas comes but once a year,
And when it comes it brings good cheer.

As I ponder again the course of the seasons and the coming of Christmas, I fall to thinking of the spirit of cheerfulness, but also upon the contrary spirit, the haunting evil that is in the world today, casting shadow and whispering alarm.

"Be of good cheer," said Jesus, and again, "Fear not, I am the first and the last."

The dark and the light, the negative and the positive, the defeated and the victorious, are in these contrasted biblical words, "fear" and "cheer." Taking the words literally, the Bible refers more often to fears than to cheers, yet, undoubtedly, the predominant note of the Christian faith and message is all on the side of the cheers. Our generation is too familiar with the fear complex. Fear bestrides the five continents and sails the seven seas.

There is the fear arising from the almost universal lowering of the moral currency. When men cannot trust each other, when the spoken word is unreliable, bonds are depreciated and pledges are debased, suspicions multiply, looks are sly and furtive, jealousies and envies are increased, and insecurity breeds fears.

Recession from faith is another prime cause of fear. When men no longer say, "Thy rod and Thy staff they comfort me," they lack that confidence and hope which formerly strengthened the heart and carried their fathers over the rough roads and the high hills of life. This generation is discovering that Christian faith, as practiced by the sturdy believers of earlier days, was not just a delightful sentiment or a social convention. Faith is an indispensable element in successful living. When faith is neglected or abandoned, all human values fall. Evict faith from the house of life, and you will be burgled and ruined by predatory fears. Neglect of God carries with it its own punishment, and the God-forgetting man must confess with the poet:

> *Still behind me steps I hear*
> *Of my life-companion, fear!*
> *From myself that fear has grown,*
> *And the shadow is my own.*

"We have our fingers crossed until 1952," said a New York businessman to me. He was referring to economic fears—the sensitivity of the money market, the perils of international exchange of money and goods, the risks of business, the rise and fall of investments, the uncertain wealth of men and nations. In such things are the breeding grounds of highly dangerous fears. When recurrent wars destroy material assets, the survivors become avid for their share in what is left, hungry desires are born and are stimulated by shortage and new strifes ensue.

Jeremiah referred to a "voice of trembling, of fear, and not of peace." The same tones are heard today as new clashes and discords break the comity of nations. We are beset by fears of renewed and more terrible strife.

The toiler, the wage earner, fears that his work may fail, his slender savings collapse when banks and credits totter. He fears that the house he is buying may prove too much for his purse and the mortgagor foreclose on him. The young couple, looking toward the marriage altar, fear that war and misfortune may make a cruel jest of their happy dreams. The young mother feels apprehensive as she sees her baby boy begin to walk, and wonders whether he will one day go away while the drums and marching footsteps beat a mournful tattoo in her desolate heart.

Who can wonder at these extraordinary fears of ordinary people? Can we so soon forget the mechanical slaughter of a generation?

There is no doubt that fear is one of our stronger emotions. A certain amount of it is essential to a balanced character. Without it a sense of responsibility is lacking, and there are elements in evidence of rashness, hardness, cruelty and improvidence.

We learn from the Bible that "the fear of the Lord is the beginning of wisdom." We are urged to "pass the time of your sojourning here in fear" (1 Peter 1:17). Fear carried to excess plays a large part in primitive religion, but properly enlightened, it becomes awe and reverence. These are qualities we do well to cultivate.

It is when fear is without God, and carried to excess, that it becomes the bane of our emotions and tyrannizes over the will. Against this kind of fear the Bible often warns us, and we are told that such "fear hath torment."

Men are so conscious of fear that they have a whole science of it. Upon these classified terrors we will not dwell, but they range from the childish fear of the dark to the victims of pantophobia—fear of everything.

Since fears are so destructive of human happiness we naturally look for a true antidote. To fight it by direct assault, to cast it out by main force is not a success. The more you strive to drive it out, the more successfully you seem to drive it in! Even prayer about fear may sometimes become merely a sublimated anxiety, lacking the secret of true repose in God.

Spiritual strategy requires both a Presence and a glorious truth to be introduced to cancel and drive out fear. The Psalmist cried, "I will fear no evil, for thou art with me!" And again, "The Lord is my salvation: whom shall I fear?"

Jesus came to us with the message, "Fear not." And we do well at this Christmas season to remember that the Gospels give us three "good cheers." They all come direct from Jesus to our fear-stricken hearts. What wonderful Christmas gifts, if only we will accept them!

"Be of good cheer. Thy sins be forgiven thee." Sins forgiven mean no more tax of suffering and fear upon the conscience.

"Be of good cheer: it is I ... Be not afraid," conveys an assurance of a Living Presence in whose light fears cannot live.

"Be of good cheer: I have overcome the world." God has the first and the last word— "Fear not ..."

Ring the bells! Sing the carols! Exchange gifts! Kneel at the cradle!

A happy Christmas to you one and all. I give you "good cheer."

48

My First Christmas in Christ

Jerome Hines
1957

It was early in November of 1954. I was walking down Broadway in New York City on my way to a rehearsal at the Metropolitan Opera Company. Suddenly my eye caught sight of a display of Christmas cards in one of the store windows.

"Oh, brother!" I muttered. "Christmas again."

Quickly I began calculating in my mind the mountain of things I had to do before December 25th. Why, the thought of Christmas cards alone was enough to stagger me. There would be at least 200 cards for the personnel and staff of the Met, plus an almost endless list of concert managers across the country, plus several scores of personal friends, plus—

I stopped myself short.

"Well, Jerry," I said to myself. "That's a great way to think about the Savior's birthday. You ought to be thinking of how you can put Christ into Christmas this year, not of all the burdens the season imposes."

The more I thought about it, the more I realized that for me the sending of Christmas cards had been purely a matter of business. It had nothing at all to do with Christ. I realized that, as a Christian of just a few weeks standing, I would have to change my attitude and readjust my thinking.

I began concrete action that night when I got home. I suggested to my wife and my mother that we forget sending Christmas cards and give the money we would ordinarily spend to the Army's Bowery Corps to help provide dinners for the men of Skid Row.

We went to that dinner—my wife Lucia and I. And to a party given by the Army for the men at the Bowery.

I had sung in the services a number of times before that Christmas Day. But I felt apart from the men. I had never spoken to them, either individually or as a group. To me they had been little more than a sea of faces, almost inhuman.

After eating Christmas dinner with the men that day, I went and helped the major pass out gifts to the men. For the first time the congregation "came alive." Suddenly there came to me the realization that they are human—just like the men you find in any part of the world and in any walk of life.

That experience was like the breaking of a shell. Hearing the men say "Thank you" for my songs and "God bless you" gave me courage, made me feel as though I belonged.

For the first time that day I realized I belonged to the great Christian family. Instead of God merely being a part of me, I was a part of God! I was a brother of Christ and a co-laborer with Him.

That first Christmas in Christ was almost as big a turning point in my life as the day I knelt at the altar and accepted Christ as my Savior. That day I stopped being *only* a singer—I became a useful part of the Bowery. Christ belonged to me, and I belonged to Him—completely.

Christmas in Bethlehem

Commissioner W. R. H. Goodier
1981

The tour party approached Bethlehem with anticipation. Would it be anything like we had imagined?

It came in sight. There it was—a town of about 300 souls 2,000 years ago, now with 30,000 inhabitants, located on a rocky hill about 2,600 feet above sea level and five miles south of Jerusalem.

We were now entering the village mentioned in the first book of the Bible, for here Rachel died and was buried (Genesis 35:19). Here Ruth met Boaz and married him. In Bethlehem David was born and anointed king of Israel by the prophet Samuel (1 Samuel 16:1-4). But that was not why we had come, nor why countless millions visit this little town, nor the reason for Christmas pilgrimages.

The town has become immortal, for here was Jesus born. It is the birthplace of Christianity.

The same town, but different. Time has a way of changing most things. For instance we approached, not riding a disgruntled donkey or on foot, but traveling in an air-conditioned coach. There is still evidence of antiquity, the ancient architecture, the influence of that early culture, but also the modern and the inevitable commercialization.

Our first stop was one such place, a shop of souvenirs—a tourist trap, we were to discover. But at least before they turned us loose to spend our money they led us to the rooftop where the guide pointed out to us the very fields on the Judean hills where it is believed the shepherds tended their flocks on that first Christmas.

For centuries the sheep that had served as sacrifices for the altar in the Temple of Jerusalem had pastured there in those hills, about three miles east of Bethlehem. It was there David had shepherded the flocks. On this occasion our thoughts naturally turned to Luke 2:

And there were in the same country shepherds abiding in the field, keeping watch over their flocks by night. And, lo, the angel of the Lord came upon them, and the glory of the Lord shone round about them: and they were sore afraid. And the angel said unto them, Fear not: for, behold, I bring you good tidings of great joy, which shall be to all people. For unto you is born this day in the city of David a Savior, which is Christ the Lord.

In due time we were taken to see the place we were all so anxious to see. Our bus drove down Manger Street headed for the Church of the Nativity and pulled into the parking lot across from the church. It is a large basilica, built in the shape of a cross 170 feet long and 80 feet wide, directly over the spot where Jesus was born.

The architecture and the materials used were not where my interest lay, though much history was represented—a mosaic from the fourth century left from the Crusader wall decoration, and wood carvings of the Nativity made from the cedars of Lebanon.

Our interest focused on the Grotto of the Nativity, the place where God took human form. It is a cave, rectangular in shape, 35 feet by 10 feet, accessed by a small entrance through which we passed one by one. Inside, in a niche in the wall there has been inlaid in the stone floor a silver star with a Latin inscription: *Hic de Virgine Maria Jesus Christus natus est* (Here Jesus Christ was born of the Virgin Mary). Unbelievable! To think we were there on the very spot, the sacred place where Christ was born! Mrs. Goodier and I had our picture taken to recall the moment.

To the right of that spot where Jesus was born is the manger. It is thought to have been used to store the fodder, a place nice and dry, and much more comfortable for the baby than to be laid on the hard ground. We naturally recalled the words:

And she brought forth her firstborn son, and wrapped him in swaddling clothes, and laid him in a manger; because there was no room for them in the inn (Luke 2:7).

While we were there a young couple came with their little infant. With loving care they took the baby and placed him in the manger where Jesus had lain, and prayed. It was an act of worship, of dedication. It became easy to imagine the Christ Child lying in that very place all those years ago.

We left that place, our eyes misty with tears, our hearts brimming with emotion. As the bus drove on and we traversed the road winding up between the City of David and the "Holy City" we did not feel like indulging in idle chatter. As we reflected on what we had seen I became aware of the short distance from Bethlehem to Jerusalem—how near the cross to the cradle. Between the cities I thought, here we are in the carefully selected setting for the jewel of the greatest price. Here was the stage on which was portrayed the greatest love story of all time:

For God so loved the world, that He gave His only begotten Son, that whosoever believeth in Him should not perish, but have everlasting life (John 3:16).

Love begets love. Such amazing love invites my love in return. With Christina G. Rossetti we say:

What can I give Him,
Poor as I am?
If I were a shepherd,
I would give Him a lamb,
If I were a Wise Man,
I would do my part—
But what can I give Him,
Give my heart.

Somehow this Christmas is different for those of us who visited Bethlehem. In our memory we stand on those shepherds' hills, and hear the song of the angels: *Glory to God in the highest, and on earth peace, goodwill toward men* (Luke 2:14).

It is with new feeling and greater understanding that we sing:

O holy Child of Bethlehem,
*   Descend to us, we pray;*
Cast out our sins, and enter in,
*   Be born in us today.*
We hear the Christmas angels
*   The great glad tidings tell,*
O come to us, abide with us,
*   Our Lord Emmanuel.*

A Mouse and A Tune

Doris Harris
1969

He was hungry. It was cold in the old church, and he was looking for something to eat. His tiny bright eyes widened and his whiskers twitched. Then he began to eat.

The bellows of the old organ gave him many a delicious meal that fall and early winter of 1818.

He'd always liked being a church mouse. His friends who lived in townhouses or inns or ancient castles often came to visit him. He decided that they came when they needed peace and quiet, as they knew when to avoid the day when the church was packed with people and the ancient organ made a huge, ugly sound. And what's more, churches didn't usually have cats.

So when his friends came to visit, he let them sleep long and deeply and shared his meager larder with them. But this had been a hard fall and winter. And he had needed the organ bellows.

He could tell from the bells and the snow and the pine decorations in the church that it was nearing Christmas. He looked forward to it because he had heard there was food in the building after that day.

The air was crisp and cold, and he was nibbling hard at the bellows when the great door opened. He scampered into his hole and watched.

He relaxed. He knew this good man, Josef Mohr, who preached to the people. With him was the schoolmaster. His most nervous friend, the schoolhouse mouse, said it was very nerve-racking, what with the noise and the pet cats fol-lowing the children to school and the children throwing things at him and chasing him if he ventured out of his hole.

The two men were talking. Then one sat down at the old organ.

"Oh! Oh!" thought the mouse, remembering his organ-bellows meals.

Sure enough, the old organ couldn't wheeze a sound.

"Let's take a look," the pastor said, creeping around the organ. "Look here! The bellows have been eaten right through!"

"Even the mice are hungry in Salzburg this year," said the schoolmaster. "It promises to be a sad Christmas. It's cold. The peasants and barge-men are already hungry, and now there'll be no music for the Christmas Eve service."

The little mouse was sad. He hadn't meant to ruin Christmas.

He watched the two sad-faced men sit down with their faces buried in their hands.

Music? He thought about the strange instrument that stood behind a door. Once when he had run by, it had fallen with a *pling* sound.

He moved quickly to the instrument. He ran by it as hard as he could. But it didn't move. He ran by it again. This time he bumped it and it moved ever so slightly. The fourth time, it started sliding to the floor, and he jumped out of sight.

P-l-l-l-l-i-n-g!

He peeked around the door. Both men raised their heads and looked at one another.

"What's that?"

"A guitar!"

"Guitar? A guitar here?"

"It's a musical instrument!"

"Some might call it that."

"If we can write a simple hymn tune that could be accompanied by the guitar, it would be the answer."

They went out talking excitedly.

The church mouse heard what had happened the next day from the school mouse. The two men had stayed up nearly all night writing a hymn for Christmas. They'd even had some bread late at night and the school mouse had shared the crumbs.

The church mouse huddled in his hole and smelled the fragrance of pine boughs and burning candles. The people were all there. The poor, poverty stricken people of Obendorf, Austria. The women sat in their shawls, and the children, hungry and cold, sat wide-eyed in the quiet beauty of the old church. The men sat with big, gnarled hands folded quietly as they waited for the Christmas Eve service to begin.

The church mouse felt his whiskers twitch and a little tear splashed down his long nose. He hadn't meant to cause them grief. But then he pricked up his ears as he heard the preacher's voice.

"Our organ will not play. But we have written a new Christmas hymn. I will teach you the words. Listen carefully."

There was a hush as a clear voice sang, accompanied by the guitar.

"Silent night, holy night,
All is calm, all is bright …"

When he finished they all joined in. It was the most beautiful music the mouse had ever heard.

He was almost glad that the winter had been cold and that he'd eaten the organ bellows. If he hadn't, perhaps the hymn "Silent Night" would never have been written.

You Are Invited

Commissioner Bramwell Tripp
1981

Have you been invited somewhere for Christmas? If so, you look forward happily to visiting with friends. But whether you've received an invitation from others or not, I have one for you. It was originally spoken to a small group a long time ago, but it is also for you today.

The words are those of the shepherds who saw and heard the angelic heralds. They said, "Let us now go even unto Bethlehem, and see this thing which is come to pass, which the Lord hath made known unto us" (Luke 2:15).

The invitation is to everyone. "Let *us* now go!" It had its personal aspect in that each one had to decide for himself. But neither this journey to the Bethlehem manger nor any other valid Christian experience is undertaken in solitude. We make a personal decision and then go along with others. We become part of an innumerable company who have followed after the shepherds to stand in wonder and reverence and joy at the manger cradle of the Christ Child.

The invitation is to accept now. "Let us *now* go!" The shepherds didn't waste time, as the next verse says, "they came with haste and found Mary, and Joseph, and the babe lying in a manger." Time passes quickly. We say, "It hardly seems possible that it's Christmas again." Another year has gone by. Soon we'll have one less year to live, one less Christmas to enjoy. Now is the time to make sure that this Christmas will be eternally significant.

The invitation is to act. "Let us now *go!*" It doesn't really matter whether you go in the simplicity of the shepherds or with the deliberate purposefulness of the wise men, but go! You may bend your knee in a cathedral or a chapel, or you may bow in faith and reverence before Jesus, Son of God, Savior of the world, in your own home. It may involve a position of the body or words spoken with the lips, or it may be done without visible action or audible sounds. True worship is not a matter of place or posture or pronouncement. It is an affair of the heart.

The invitation was accepted. It is said of the shepherds that they "returned, glorifying God for all the things that they had heard and seen." Will you share their experience? "Oh, come, let us adore Him, Christ the Lord!"

One of Our People

General Erik Wickberg
1972

On Christmas Day last year the commanding officer of a well-known Salvation Army corps in London gave a dinner for lonely people. Between 200 and 300 accepted his invitation and were feasted in the Army hall.

Salvationists the world over plan similar celebrations for many different kinds of people. While not every guest may be poor and needy, all are lonely, and Christmas can prove a sad occasion for those who feel themselves alone.

The day after last year's event the London officer received a telephone call from the police.

"We have found one of your people dead," the sergeant said.

"And the name?"

The Salvationist shook his head. He could bring to mind no one in his corps of that name.

"Could there be a mistake?"

"Oh, no," the sergeant said. "He was one of your people, all right. In his pocket we found a ticket to your Christmas dinner."

Yes. He was one of our people.

Once, in French-speaking Switzerland, I presided over an old folks' feast and invited a representative of the city to address the guests. He recounted that as a young student, many years earlier, he had been on a trip to Germany. A complete stranger, unable to converse in the language, he had gone for a walk on Christmas Eve.

Seeing two Salvationists in the familiar uniform, he decided to follow them. This led to an Army hall, where tables were laid for a festive meal lit by a many-candled Christmas tree.

"I did not understand a word they were saying," he remarked, "but I realized I was welcome. Never shall I forget that Christmas Eve."

Our people!

Attending a carol service at one of our girls' homes, I learned from the matron that some of the residents had lost all touch with their families. While this did not usually concern them unduly, as Christmas drew near they grew depressed at the thought that they would receive neither cards nor gifts.

More than one girl had been known to address a card to herself, even to mail a small parcel, unaware that she would be kindly remembered. The matron's custom was to give presents to all her girls.

Our people!

It was just before Christmas 1939. Three Polish submarines had fled across the Baltic during the war between Germany and Poland, seeking refuge in Swedish territorial waters. In accordance with international law, the submarines were taken into custody and the men interned in a small town outside Stockholm.

One of our Stockholm bands sought permission to visit and play to the internees. I accompanied the bandsmen. None of us could speak a word of Polish.

When the first piece of music had been rendered and enthusiastically applauded, I said a sentence in German, apologizing for not knowing their language. Could they understand me? Would they like me to try to make myself understood in that tongue?

They greeted me with loud and marked approval. It seemed evident many of them could follow my words. I expressed our good wishes and spoke of the message of Christmas—of hope, of peace, of goodwill.

Our people!

"Tidings of great joy ... to all people" was the Christmas greeting the angels proclaimed when Christ was born.

As they look upon the earth at yet another Christmastide, surely there is disappointment at the selfishness and greed on a worldwide scale that prevents our sharing what we possess with those who have less.

While praiseworthy efforts for the greater amelioration of suffering are on the way, these are not enough. Each of us, to our utmost capacity, must increasingly support publicity and pressure for much more help—much more food to starving millions, much more assistance toward self-help, toward schools, toward hospitals, and access to the latest scientific methods of food production.

In all our support of these great schemes we should not for one moment forget or, in any other way, neglect our Christian responsibility toward the individual close at hand. Our neighbor. Our people! The two concerns—worldwide and nearest to us—should ever receive equal attention in our thought and practice.

The Salvation Army has a special mission among people who are forgotten, who are lonely, who have lost hope. There are so many of them. They seem to know us; they seem to trust us. Our uniform speaks of an open door when other doors appear closed, and of a willingness to help without asking many questions.

Our people!

William Booth used to say that while he held out one hand to those who possessed this world's means and the other to those who had none, he feared that if he held on too tightly with one hand, he would lose his grip with the other.

Such a fear proves groundless when both hands are first and continually in the Master's strong and loving hand, the hand that shall never lose its grip.

Having the joy of His hand on ours, the joy that His forgiveness and His fellowship shower on our lives, our hands touched by His continually reach out, undismayed, undiscouraged, to all people. Our people. His people!

They Wrote about Christmas

Bernard Palmer
1965

More than one hundred twenty years ago Tiny Tim's bright, childish belief in the Christmas season began to teach love and generosity and the true meaning of Christmas as he softened old Scrooge's heart. With the active assistance of the ghosts of Christmas Past, Christmas Present and Christmas Yet To Come, he taught the lonely miser that Christmas is not a time of "fraud and humbug" but of kindness and the joy of God.

This year thousands of parents who as children suffered and rejoiced with Tiny Tim as they heard the story at their parents' knees, will share the same delight with their children. And sometime during the holidays Charles Dickens' "A Christmas Carol" is sure to be read over dozens of television stations and listened to as avidly as it was when Dickens himself used to read it before audiences in England and America. It has been translated into almost every known language, and millions of copies have been sold.

For centuries Christmas has challenged the imagination and provided the inspiration for thousands of writers all over the world. While the simplicity and majesty of the New Testament accounts of Christ's birth can never be equaled, there have been many memorable stories and novels that have helped to portray the true depth and spirit of Christmas.

Probably the best known of all is "A Christmas Carol." Charles Dickens was jouncing uncomfortably in a Manchester-bound train in October 1843 when suddenly the idea came to him.

"It came with such clarity and force," he said, "that I hurried back to London from my lecture as quickly as possible to get it down on paper."

Although the idea came quickly, the story was not easily written. Dickens worked long and hard at it, writing, striking out and writing again. The original manuscript bears numerous alterations and marginal additions in his own handwriting.

The publisher got "A Christmas Carol" printed in time for Christmas of 1843. The six-thousand-copy first edition was sold out in a single day at five shillings (about one dollar) each. Second and third editions were sold out quickly to bring the total sales to fifteen thousand copies in a few weeks. Several years later Dickens included the "Carol" in a Christmas issue of his magazine which had a circulation of two hundred fifty thousand copies. In the United States more than two million copies of "A Christmas Carol" in book form have been sold, and it is still selling well.

Although Dickens was always popular in America, none of his works received more acclaim than "A Christmas Carol." When he traveled America lecturing and giving selected readings, "A Christmas Carol" was a great favorite.

In 1868 he wrote a friend of one experience: "I have got to know the 'Carol' so well that I can't remember it and occasionally go dodging about in the wildest manner to pick up lost pieces. They took it so tremendously last night that I was stopped for five minutes."

The year after Dickens wrote "A Christmas Carol" he tried his hand at the subject with a story entitled "The Chimes." It concerned those who were poor and underprivileged and their right to happiness. A year later he turned out still a third Christmas story, "The Cricket on the Hearth." The last two efforts were interesting and had a certain following, but they lacked the magic that has made "A Christmas Carol" grip the hearts of each successive generation. Today few people have ever heard of them.

Legends have long had a place in our heritage, and Christmas is no exception. Newspapers and magazines often reprint Selma Lagerlof's legend "The Holy Night" as Christmas approaches. In it the aged grandmother, left home with the little girl while the rest of the family goes to church, tells the story to her.

"But that which is needful," she concludes, "is that we have such eyes as can see God's glory."

The Swedish Nobel Prize winner also wrote the delightful "Legend of the Christmas Rose." It recounts the adventures of Abbott Hans and his associate when they visit the robber family in Goinge Forest and see the great forest burst into glorious bloom on Christmas Eve. It is the story of one man's great faith and the lovely flower, the Christmas Rose, which came to stand as its symbol.

Washington Irving takes us back to another day in "The Sketchbook." With his masterful pen he strokes in vivid accounts of old English Christmas customs. We feel the solidity of home and family the joys to be found in simple things. We are inspired to cut away the froth and tinsel from our own Christmas observance and to bring it back to the simple enjoyment of family and close friends.

In these days of crass materialism, the sacrifice of O. Henry's "Gift of the Magi" still touches hearts with its tender expression of love. Few can read it without gaining a little better understanding that the true spirit of Christmas is giving, not receiving. Readers are stirred by Christopher Morley's story of "The Tree That Didn't Get Trimmed."

Children, with their sense of fitness and imagery, are delighted with Hans Christian Andersen's fable of the fir tree.

Henry van Dyke also wrote about a tree. "The First Christmas Tree" sharply defines the purpose of Christmas as being to observe the birth of Christ, who came to free men from the chains of paganism. In the story Winfried, an early missionary to Germany, cuts down the great oak sacred to a pagan god as a human being is about to be sacrificed on Christmas Eve, and he dedicates a young fir tree to the Christ Child in its stead.

The Nativity itself has long intrigued the writers of every land. Pageants and plays and stories describing that great event continue to pour from the presses as they have in times past. Fictionalized accounts of Christ's birth have been told and retold as seen through the eyes of Mary, Joseph, each of the wise men and the shepherds. One such story relates what happened as seen by one of the oxen tied in the stable.

The Nativity is the theme of the short novel, *The Story of the Other Wise Man*, written by Henry van Dyke. The Bible account does not say how many magi actually came to see Christ, stating only "there came wise men from the east." Following the traditional account that there were three, van Dyke tells the story of the fourth wise man. He starts out with the others to find the Christ Child and journeys part way with them. However he stops on the way to help those in need.

Before leaving on his journey he sells everything he owns and buys three exquisite jewels for gifts to the King for whom he is searching. He guards them jealously until he sees a man lying along the roadside. Although his companions are so anxious to see the King that they hurry on, the fourth wise man stops and eventually uses the sapphire to pay for the ill man's needs. He is hopeful of catching up with the others, but caring for the stranger takes so long that he arrives in Bethlehem late.

The three wise men have already made their visit and have departed; and Joseph, Mary and Jesus have fled to the safety of Egypt. Dejectedly he walks the streets of Bethlehem. There he meets the soldiers sent out by Herod to kill all the children under two years of age. Using the second jewel, a beautiful ruby, he is able to save the life of one of the children.

Although he only has one gift left, he goes on and on, searching for the King he has not been able to find. For thirty-three years he wanders about through many lands, always hopeful that he will find Him, but never doing so.

At last the "other wise man," now gray and bent with age, makes his way to Jerusalem at the time of the Passover. There he sees a young girl who is being sold into slavery. Using his last gift, a large pearl, he buys the freedom of the girl.

Although the last of his gifts is gone, he finds the King at Golgotha, where He is being crucified. A voice tells him, "Inasmuch as thou hast done it unto one of the least of these my brethren, thou hast done it unto me."

But the story is more than just a lesson in doing good. It links Christ's birth with His death, the stable with the Cross.

The "Other Wise Man," too, is becoming a tradition on television. But, whether it is read or watched, it is a powerful, moving story that touches the hearts of men.

There are novels and essays and stories that tell of Christmas and what the season ought to mean to each of us. We would do well to read them and heed their message that we ought to be kind and generous and gracious, even as Christ was. They tell that He was born at Christmas for the express purpose of dying on the Cross to save us from sin.

But as we are busy with our reading, let us not forget the account as written by Luke. It is the most beautiful and amazing story in all the world.

Adore Him

General Evangeline Booth
1948

Adoration for Christ is the divine vitality that everywhere produces and restores life.

Jesus came to the world an infant. He could have come a king, escorted by a retinue of the angelic host, resplendent with evidences of regal power which would have made the world proud to receive Him.

But He entered our race at its lowest point. He gave divine appeal to weakness at its weakest. He glorified the cradle. He ennobled boyhood. He sanctified motherhood. He took upon Himself humanity through that influence which is the most powerful in its approach to the human heart—that of a little child.

Nor did His surroundings recommend Him. The stable and the manger were anything but regal. The Wise Men, having been led by a Star of such significance, were given to think they would find the child in surroundings of splendor. It must have been a shock when they were directed to the dilapidated barn with its shabby, drab walls, its uneven stone floor and the crude hewn manger, all so unlike the Star and the angels' song.

I am glad the Wise Men were not so blinded by their learning that they refused to follow the

directions and missed Him. It is hard to dismiss all idea of finding Christ in preconceived surroundings of intellectual splendor and to look for Him in sacrifice and perhaps in tears.

Adoration begins with a question because its birth is in the mind. To think that its origin is in the heart is a mistake. It is our conception of a thing that makes it desirable. One person says the girl is pretty, the picture wonderful, the house beautiful. Another say, "I don't see the girl to be pretty; the picture to me is without meaning; I wouldn't live in the house."

It is thought that creates desire for possession. And the generator of thought is the brain. Its forces are tremendous. Men are guilty when they act without its authority. Emotions may sometimes forsake us, but thought, under their power transmuted into word or action, is immortal.

Who can doubt an infinite Creator when He gave to Man the intellect with its incomparable powers? Its miraculous revolutions swinging the mind from the farthest recesses of the past to the utmost limits of the future quicker than the eye can blink or the clock can tick! The scales in which we weigh life's ever-arising questions and adjust their legitimate proportions from the balances of thought! The eye which sees what is not and from its mental vision works it out to be! The tenacious hand which holds what is not there to grasp, yet holds until it shapes its object into a tangible form! The intellect! God's stamp upon His handiwork, lifting Man above the beast. God's masterpiece of creation, tracing in the human the image of the divine.

When God gave man his brain, He gave him a boat, a sail and a rudder. It is according to the set of the sails what shore he makes. So many are not attracted to good because they never *think* good. They do evil because they *think* evil—dwell upon its false investments and try to be happy in its disappointing returns.

But mighty as the brain is, it is a weak instrument when substituting for the heart. It is the heart leaning over the cradle that fascinates me. All through my life I have found it to be the heart that wins. It is by love we conquer. And when the heart ceases to love, it has ceased to live.

Knowledge will never take the place of love. *Knowing* is nothing to *being*. No amount of learning provides devotion. Perfect information cannot and will not control action. Familiarity with the Ten Commandments is powerless to keep them. The difference between the service of love and the service of duty is immeasurable. The service of love may be imperfect in expression and lacking in culture, whereas the service of duty in obedience to a regulation may be perfect in conformation to rule and order. The service required to meet the demand of a moral obligation, a promise, or to answer the claims of conscience is praiseworthy and correct. But the difference between it and the service of love is the difference between a tumbler of water from the kitchen faucet on a scorching hot day and of catching in a crude goblet the icy stream as it rushes down its mountain path to the sea.

In the service of duty the price and the reward are considered. In the service of love, the sweat of the brow, the tears, the toils, the hidden sacrifices do not count. We are absorbed in the passion of adoration, and adoration thirsts only for greater opportunity to express itself.

The shepherds and the Wise Men sought the Babe with every energy allowed to search. Becoming confused as to the road had no power to turn them back. The Star and the song had told them He was there, and nothing would suffice but to find Him.

How many see the Star, join in the hymns, give to the Church or the Army, get quite a distance along the road, but fail to reach the stable. Sorrow comes, dissatisfaction with the treasures of life, or some overwhelming temptation. They know then they have never really found Him.

I like this expression, *adore*. In it there is the abandonment of passion, total disdain of measurement, a throwing away of scales, a wholesale destruction of tape-lines. I like this. By nature I am a totalitarian in demands upon myself. I cannot do things in part. I must do them wholly. This has got me into some troubles, but it has helped me to give, to suffer, to sacrifice—sacrifice readily, in fact eagerly—a thousand times ten thousand, and sacrifice is never without its crowning.

Passion is the elixir of life. Without passion, religion, history, romance and art are withered leaves, for passion is the great mover and spring of the soul. Why should it be such an indispensable adjunct in sport, in business, in music, in learning and in art and not be necessary in religion, when Christ is the central fact of the Christian system and all our religion was born of the Crib and the Cross?

I was at the Klondike and saw the passion of men for gold. I was in the Ottawa fire and saw the passion of husbands for wives, of mothers for children and parents. I was in the San Francisco earthquake and saw the passion of men for life. *Why not the heat, the endurance, the sacrificial beauty of passion in religion?*

Upon its wing we touch the highest point of devotion. In the throes of its fires, we make the most daring attacks. Clothed in its armor we can overcome the bitterest foe.

Adoration is the expression of the soul's passion for Christ. It gives beauty to everything. It did with the mother of Jesus. It lit up the old barn and made it the most renowned piece of architecture in the world's history. It was the ineffable beauty in the mother's face, denoting completeness of surrender to the Child's good. It gave divine exaltation to the Wise Men and expectant wonderment to the shepherds, while it broke down all barriers between the learned and the untaught, the man of high estate and the man of the shepherd's crook.

O Little Child of Bethlehem, we will give to Thee that adoration that gives with the recklessness of the thoughtless prodigal and then fears it has not given enough.

War Cry cover, 1955: artist unknown

Come Into Our World

Photo: Robin Bryant, 1996

All around us, seemingly,
Darkness holds its sway;
Truth and love are faltering,
Peace in disarray;

And if we needed You,
We need You now!
Come into our world
Come into our world,
O Come now, Lord Jesus!

People sit in loneliness,
Children cry for bread;
Men fight men in hatred,
By suspicion led;

And if we needed You,
We need You now!
Come into our world
Come into our world,
O Come now, Lord Jesus!

Faced with such confusion,
Hope has slipped away;
Men have stopped believing,
Forgotten how to pray;

And if we needed You,
We need You now!
Come into our world
Come into our world,
O Come now, Lord Jesus!

—Joy Webb, 1996

Now and Here

What profit should we win the race
To solve the mysteries of space
And send new suns and satellites
To signal through ten thousand nights,
If we neglect to read the Star
Shining forever from afar
On Jesus, cradled from His birth
On the dark bosom of the Earth?

And what are victories of skill
Unless, exploring in God's will,
We prove the Law we there have found
In this our world, our Holy ground?
For God is NOW and God is HERE,
Not hidden in some shadowy sphere.
Who stoops to heed another's cry
Shall touch His hand and reach the sky.

—Catherine Baird, 1969

War Cry cover, 1962: Charles F. Horndorf

War Cry back cover, 1986: Joni Eareckson Tada

O Little Town of Bethlehem

Joni Eareckson Tada
1993

What one of us hasn't gone Christmas caroling at one time or another—maybe to a nursing home or a nearby hospital. Maybe you bundled up and wore jackets and huddled outside of some neighbor's house and sang carols. Perhaps you invited some friends over to your house for hot cider and pumpkin pie and Christmas hymns sung around the piano.

Well, looking back on my childhood, I have some very special memories of going Christmas caroling with my family. My family has always been into horses. And I remember going Christmas caroling on horseback, of all things.

Now, I couldn't have been more than four or five years old at the time, up on top of that big, old horse of mine. We galloped to a nearby farmhouse and pulled our horses up outside of the neighbor's front door, got out our hymnals from our saddlebags and sang those beautiful choruses. You can imagine it gets pretty cold on those dark winter nights. That's when my father would pull out hot water bottles from his saddle bags and put them between us and the cold seat of our saddles. What a way to warm up!

But, you know, more than just the memory of night-time horseback rides through snow and the cold, the most wonderful part for me were those beautiful Christmas carols. Now, my favorite way back then was "O Little Town of Bethlehem"—especially the line that says, "O little town of Bethlehem, how still we see thee lie, Above thy deep and dreamless sleep, the silent stars go by."

I love the picture that paints.

Even though I was just a child, the words of that carol described the beautiful picture in my mind of what that silent, starry night must have been like.

Those were days long ago and far away for me. But "O Little Town of Bethlehem" is still a seasonal favorite of mine. There are other words in that carol now, though, that hold a far deeper meaning for me. I especially like that last line to the hymn, "O holy Child of Bethlehem, descend on us we pray; Cast out our sin and enter in, be born in us today."

Wow, serious words for a Christmas carol, don't you think? You see, that line in the song minces no words, does it? Jesus isn't simply a baby that we adore in a cradle somewhere. You know, He's not simply someone to whom we sing carols or celebrate with gifts or family gatherings. Christ had a purpose in coming. And Christmas has meaning because of those words. "Jesus, cast out our sin and enter in. Be born in us today."

When I was a child, even though the Christmas memories were very precious to me, I'm not so sure I caught the full meaning behind the birth of Christ. Ah, but now I know—thank God, I know. And I trust that in this season you understand also. May the Christ we worship enter your heart today—casting out any sin that stands in the way. And if you don't know Him already, may He be born in you today.

Reprinted with permission of JAF Ministries, P.O. Box 3333, Agoura Hills, CA 91301; www.jafministries.com.

Make Christmas for Someone

Brigadier Christine McMillan
1980

"Come out, everyone and see the pine grove! You'll never see it looking so beautiful."

It was the day before Christmas and to our joy it had snowed heavily the night before, and even now the frosty air was full of lazily turning feathery flakes.

As we stepped into the fragrant stillness of the pine grove, a shaft of silver sunlight pierced the heavy snowladen clouds. Instantly every branch and feathery twig was aglitter with a million lights—all save one tree. Its dark green branches bore no lovely snow blossoms; it gave forth no glittering sparkle. Quiet and grave it stood in the wood, withdrawn and strangely lovely in its dark beauty.

It reminds me that amid all the delicious bustle and thrilling excitement of Christmas there are hearts that are sorrowful. The colorful wrappings, the gay cards, the plans for the great day, and even the Christmas music, have little meaning for them.

Perhaps loneliness has camped on their doorstep. In all the great city, there is none who calls them friend. There are no exciting invitations to dinner, no gifts, no one to whom they may even send a card.

Perhaps you are surrounded by loving friends, each one outdoing the other in attempts to help you forget the sorrow that walks with you. Last Christmas the one you loved was part of the Christmas plans. This year you are alone, and all the glitter and shimmer and breathless plans are a bitterness and a mockery to your spirit.

Perhaps you are a shut-in. Or it may be that you are part of that sad community to be found within prison walls, with a special sort of misery for company that only you know.

Well, whatever your sadness, Christmas, if you let it, can make even the darkest clouds sparkle with light. For one of the lovely things about Christmas is that its greatest warmth and light

and beauty come to us not in being done to, but in doing.

Wherever we are, our salvation lies in two things. First, to find healing in God's great love, revealed to us at Christmastime in the Child of the manger. And second, to make Christmas for someone else.

We may have no means, in the ordinary sense of the word, to make Christmas, but tinsel and ornaments and cards and gifts are not the only expressions of love. A sincere word of kindness; a sharing of something we may have, however small, with someone who has nothing; a Merry Christmas, said with a real, warm smile—these are little things, but they will mean so much to someone else.

And for that inner comfort which we must all have, or the season is cold and meaningless, let us remember the words of an unknown poet:

Souls who are sorrowful, come to the Manger
One who can comfort you waits there to bless;
One who can lead you through peril and danger,
Heal all your sorrows, and soothe your distress.

He, in the silence of midnight descending,
Speaks through earth's silence His message of peace,
Into earth's darkness His glory is sending,
Whispers to captives His word of release.

Still the glad tidings of love and salvation
Bring to the weary a promise of rest;
Low at His cradle in deep adoration,
Wait for His blessing and you shall be blessed.

Ellipses and Circles

General Frederick Coutts
1967

Great is the mystery of godliness: God was manifest in the flesh …
—1 Timothy 3:16

Small use writing a pretty-pretty piece about the lights in Oxford Street or the decorations in Bourke Street when we face the fact of the Incarnation—the Word made flesh.

This is not because I am a curmudgeon or a square. My only reason for avoiding the West End at Christmas time is that to be caught in a traffic jam is not my favorite way of spending a leisure hour. And nothing would give me greater pleasure than to walk down Bourke Street again, for it has never been my lot to be in Melbourne over Christmas. But Christmas does not center around any of the multitudinous actions of men but rather the greatest of the acts of God—His coming to earth in Christ in the form of a servant and in fashion as a man.

Scholars have pointed out that the word great in "Great is the mystery ..." means "of great importance," not difficult to understand. All the same, we had better take it both ways. Undoubtedly of great importance, but undoubtedly difficult to understand as well. As William Temple used to say, "If any man says that he understands the relation of deity to humanity in Christ, he only makes it clear that he does not understand at all what is meant by the Incarnation." Great is the mystery!

A truth can be mysterious, however, and still valid. I must not say that what I do not understand is therefore not true. The limits of human knowledge are not the final limits of reality. And because neither I nor anyone else can explain the coming of God in Christ to the world, that is no reason for saying that here is one more fairy tale—the most fanciful of the lot—which decorates that ancient fantasy called the Christian faith.

Maybe we have started at the wrong end in thinking about the divine humanity of the Redeemer. To our imperfect understanding of God we have added our imperfect understanding of our own human nature and have supposed that the addition of these two imperfections could account for the perfection of Jesus.

But whatever Jesus is, He is not the summation of our ignorance. It is true that I can better understand my own nature in the light of His, but I do not more fully understand His nature in the light of my own. Mine illuminates nothing in its own right. Every virtue I possess is derivative. While Jesus is rightly called the firstborn among many brethren, I cannot therefore deduce what He is from what I am, child though I be by grace of that same family of God of which He is the Elder Brother.

We can call the tyro emerging from the clubhouse with a new and unused set of irons a golfer, and we also call Jack Nicklaus a golfer—but there the resemblance ends. The topped drives and mangled divots of the beginner provide no clue to the skills of the professional. Jesus Christ was "truly and properly man"—as we are men, but here again the resemblance ends. What I am is small clue to what He was. We are in a dead end and will have to start again.

We may do better and go farther by recalling what was the announced intention of Jesus while He was on earth. This is common knowledge; it was to do the will of the Father. By contrast, we ourselves can have manifold interests. Like the demoniac we can answer: we are many. Competing passions war within us. With Jesus there was but one overruling desire.

An ellipse is described about two foci; a circle around one. The nearer those focal points to one another, the nearer the ellipse approaches a circle; the farther apart, the greater the difference. When the foci coincide, the ellipse becomes a circle.

The divine humanity of Jesus is most clearly seen in the realm of the will. His life on earth had but one center—the fulfilling of His Father's will. Both circles coincided, for both had a common center. Here was a mutual agreement of purpose which held good in all weathers.

In the person of Jesus, God and man were joined in the unity of a common end. When Jesus entered human life, God entered. What Jesus did, God was doing. What Jesus suffered, God suffered. God was in Christ, was the apostolic explanation. In Jesus we see God; in Jesus we also see man—both joined in the dedicated unity of a single being.

Great is the mystery! I couldn't agree more. But mystery is neither falsehood nor illusion because it happens to be mystery. The mystery of the Incarnation is a truth with which we are left to wrestle, but morning light will disclose, as it did for Jacob, the name and nature of the glorious Adversary.

Christian teachers have never denied that such doctrines as those of the Incarnation, the Atonement and the Resurrection are mysteries of which our understanding cannot be other than incomplete. Yet to know in part is still to know—which is entirely different from being led up the garden path. Even partial knowledge is some assurance that we are not the victims of a delusion. It is the shallow river whose bed can easily be seen. The deep lake in the Alps holds inviolate the secret of her soundings. Yet those depths are as real as the shallows.

At Christmas we are in the deepest of deep waters. But though this act of God in Christ transcends our understanding, faith returns grateful thanks to Him for His unspeakable gift of a Savior. Acceptance of this truth can turn any man's holiday into an unforgettable holy day.

Make Room in Your Heart

Nancy M. Armstrong
1967

Audrey watched from the big picture window as ten little girls tumbled from the station wagon and raced each other up her walk. The sight of Jan Jensen in the lead brought a pain to her heart.

They had spent many happy hours together, Jan and she. That was until she could no longer enjoy someone else's child.

Audrey opened the door to admit the noisy junior girls, wishing at once she had said "No" when Susan asked if they could practice the carols in her home.

"You're the only one close by who has a piano," Susan had said. "They're decorating the church Saturday morning and I'd have a terrible time keeping the children's attention on the songs."

"Too late to back out now," Audrey told herself as Susan shepherded the children into the living room. Suddenly her eye caught Jan's provocative grin at her elbow.

"Where's your Christmas tree?" the child demanded. "We've got ours in the window."

"We haven't a tree," Audrey said simply, and would have continued but Jan interrupted her.

"Well, you'd better hurry and get one." Jan held up fat fingers. "It's only four more days until Santa Claus comes!"

Audrey turned to help the children off with their coats and her eyes met Susan's. "I hope we're not keeping you from your Christmas preparations," Susan said, glancing around the room. "I have my house decorated, but I've a million other things to do," she added with a sigh.

"You're not keeping me from anything." Audrey's voice sounded harsh. She made a real effort to soften her tone. "Make yourselves at home; I'll be in the den if you want me."

With that she shut the door and took up her favorite place in the maple rocker. Pressing her hands to throbbing temples, she closed her eyes as if to shut out the surroundings. No, they weren't keeping her from getting ready for Christmas. There wasn't any reason to get ready. She wished the whole business of Christmas were over. And last Christmas had been so different ...

"Away in a manger, no crib for a bed ..."

The words coming from the other room stabbed at her heart. How could Susan let the children sing that song in this house? There was a crib up in the attic somewhere with ruffles and pillows she had made herself ... But there was no baby to put in it. Harry had moved the crib from the bedroom before he brought her home from the hospital. Poor Harry, she hadn't even thanked him.

"The little Lord Jesus lay down His sweet head ..."

Audrey rose from the chair and began pacing the floor. Surely a young woman like Susan with three healthy youngsters could not possibly understand the utter frustration that surged through her.

She and Harry were not young when they married but they were very much in love and full of expectancy as they bought this roomy house in the suburbs. There would be plenty of space for children and their pets and the little friends that Audrey would welcome to their home.

Four years went by—happy years spent remodeling the house, learning to garden, becoming part of a friendly community, but years filled with longing. Then the glorious day finally arrived when the doctor confirmed that she was pregnant.

Time crawled too slowly in the following months. Making more clothes than three babies needed, she had never felt happier or healthier. Everything was so right until the last few minutes in the delivery room. Then everything was so wrong. Over and over for months she had relived the nightmare of hearing the doctor's words: "I'm sorry, Mrs. Wilson, we couldn't save the baby."

The den door opened and Jan's blond head appeared around it. "Where's your bathroom, Mrs. Wilson? I forget."

"Come, I'll show you."

As they walked down the hall together Jan caught her hand. "I was the Christmas fairy in the first grade program yesterday," she said. "I had a pretty pink costume and I'm going to say the same piece in the Sunday school program. I wish you'd come."

Audrey was so conscious of the warm little hand in her own that she scarcely heard the child. She made no answer but turned on the light in the bathroom and returned to the den.

"Peace on earth, and mercy mild,
God and sinners reconciled …"

The little girls were having trouble with that one. Susan stopped playing. "You must say the words plainly so everyone will understand them. Repeat after me, 'God and sinners reconciled.'"

"Reconciled," Susan pronounced the word carefully. Ten high voices repeated it somewhat in unison.

Nice word that one, Audrey thought. Harry used it often, telling her she should become reonciled to her loss. He said she could not go on hugging grief so closely that she shut out everything and everyone else.

He had been so tender, so understanding at first, but as the months went by he had changed. Only last week he was really cross when she had told him about the woman from High Hill calling. She had brought up the subject to break the usual silence at the dinner table. Since then she had not been able to get the episode off her mind.

The young woman, Vera Coleman, had smiled warmly when she answered the doorbell. "Your friend Susan Margetts sent me to see you," she said.

Audrey had asked her in and offered her a chair, but soon regretted her act when her visitor explained that she was director of volunteer services for High Hill Home, the state training school for retarded children.

"I don't know what you have in mind, but I wouldn't be good in any capacity," Audrey had told her.

"Susan told me you've had a very difficult experience."

"It has been the biggest disappointment of my life."

"I can understand that. We lost our first baby at birth. Since then we've been blessed with two more."

"You must have been very young," Audrey remembered saying. "I'm not young … that makes it so much harder."

"I doubt very much if being young made it any easier to bear at the time." Mrs. Coleman spoke in a quiet, kindly tone. "Susan told me you taught kindergarten before your marriage. She

also told me how beautifully you helped the young people of your church to produce plays."

Audrey had been glad to help the young people with their programs. She was carrying her baby then and often thought how wonderful it would be to one day watch her own child take part.

A half smile crossed her face. "Susan is my friend and apt to be a little prejudiced in my favor."

"We're willing to take a chance on that," Vera Coleman had replied. "We desperately need help to make life less drab for children at High Hill. Many of them have parents who visit them and bring little treats, but others are forgotten by their families.

"If you could teach them games, tell stories and show those who are able how to make things, life would be so much pleasanter for them. We wouldn't expect you to come every day, but twice a week would give the children so much to look forward to."

Audrey had tried to be courteous as well as convincing, but her refusals did not get very far with Vera Coleman. "Please don't decide in a hurry. I can wait for your answer. We need you so badly."

Recalling the conversation, Audrey wondered what had possessed her to confide in this stranger and why she had ever bothered Harry with the account. He had been so enthusiastic about the project.

"Audrey, you could do it if you'd only try. There's that trunk in the attic full of your kindergarten stuff, and there's all those small instruments I helped you make for the rhythm band. The kids at High Hill would love them. The woman's right. The children would help you as much as you'd help them."

He gave her a long searching look. "Unless you make room in your heart for others you'll never be happy again." And when she had protested that Susan had no business interfering, he had startled her with his outburst.

"Susan is only trying to help you. But what's the use of any of us trying!" He had left, banging the door behind him, and Audrey had thrown herself on the bed in a fit of violent sobbing.

"Harry makes me feel like a prize heel. He just doesn't understand how I feel. Nobody does."

The children polishing off the second verse brought Audrey's thoughts back to the present.

Hail the Heaven-born Prince of Peace,
Hail the Sun of Righteousness!
Light and life to all He brings,
Risen with healing in His wings ..."

"Risen with healing in His wings," the young voices were more disciplined now and their sweetness was soothing. She hummed the line softly as they repeated it at Susan's instruction.

Healing—if only she could find that healing for her troubled spirit! Movement at the window caught her attention. A gentle snow was falling, covering the world with a blanket of peace.

How different things had been a year ago. The baby was expected a few days after Christmas. The house had been gay with decorations. Christmas Eve dinner was set on a table in front of the fireplace. Harry had come home his arms laden with brightly wrapped packages. He handed her one to unwrap, laughingly threatening her if she touched any of the others.

"A teddy bear—I figured that would do for a boy or girl," he said kissing her lightly on the tip of her nose.

After dinner she had stretched out on the lounge as Harry read his favorite Christmas passage from the Bible. The very remembrance of the occasion brought a wave of healing warmth to Audrey's heart. What was it Harry had said?

"The children would help you as much as you'd help them. Unless you make room in your heart for others ..."

All at once Audrey knew that Harry's sorrow was as deep as her own. Tears came as she realized how much she had added to his unhappiness these past months.

Walking to the desk she dialed her husband's office. "Would you mind picking up a Christmas tree on your way home?" she said hesitantly.

There was a slight pause before the answer came. "Why, I'll be glad to, dear. Anything else?"

"Yes ... Harry ... would you stop at a store for a few toys for the children at High Hill?"

The pause was longer this time. Harry cleared his throat but his voice was still husky. "Sweetheart, you've just given me the best Christmas present you possibly could. Say, wouldn't you like to help pick out the toys? I'm leaving right now ... I'll come and get you." His voice was happier than it had been in months.

Things happened fast after that. A cold drink for the carolers—they were thirsty after their long practice. The noisy bundling of ten little girls into coats and caps and mittens. Last-minute shopping with Harry and breathless preparations to catch up with Christmas.

Would she ever forget the little faces at High Hill? Audrey wondered later. No, nor the look in Harry's eyes when he told her: "Darling, there's room in that heart of yours for a whole world of children!"

The Lights Speak

Elwell Crissey
1963

Each Christmas the shining lights seem to grow brighter and more numerous. In America alone, there are literally millions! We have grown so to expect them that we cannot imagine a Christmas gloomy and dark.

Christmas illuminations have been with us for a long time, but it may not be amiss to ask some questions about them.

Do Christmas lights signify something more than pretty ornaments? Or is this Christmas radiance merely a holiday decoration, serving the same purpose as fireworks and balloons on the Fourth of July?

If there is any deeper meaning, it has been largely lost. Obviously, the majority of people now enjoying Christmas gaiety feel that the lights are simply a traditional part of the holiday. Nothing more.

Unfortunately, many Christmas celebrators scarcely remember even whose birthday is being celebrated. It is unlikely that the average person will ever bother to search the Scriptures for some esoteric meaning suggested by Christmas lights. He takes them for granted and lets it go at that.

But to do so is to miss something important.

Christmas is a unique spiritual holiday or holy day; therefore, some degree of spiritual awareness is needed to appreciate its full meaning.

Christmas lights preach a beautiful sermon, clothed in Scripture. Every careful Bible reader has noticed the exalted place which the Word assigns to light. Surely it is more than coincidence that both the New Testament and the Old Testament open with the subject of "light."

In Genesis, chapter one, it is recorded that, after heaven and earth, the first thing God created was light. And Matthew, immediately following Jesus' genealogy, quotes the wise men of the East as saying, "We have seen His star." Again, light is related to Jesus' birth when Luke writes that "the glory of the Lord shone round about" the shepherds.

Light, in Scripture, often denotes the incarnated Christ. During His ministry Jesus Himself publicly proclaimed, "I am the Light of the world." Unquestionably this was among the most stupendous claims ever made by any personality in all history. How natural, then, it must have been for medieval painters to frame every picture of Jesus, from birth to ascension, with a nimbus of light.

Since the very night Mary brought forth the Babe, special illuminations in one form or another have signaled the news of Jesus' birth. However, it was not until the fourth century that the custom of glorifying the anniversary by fire became widely observed throughout Christendom.

This marked affinity between light and Jesus provided the early Church with effective strategy against the stubborn pagan religions of Scandinavia and Northern Germany. For ages before Christian missionaries reached them, each autumn the Vikings and Goths had watched grimly as winter darkness closed around them. The day when the sun stopped its retreat, paused and started northward again, they celebrated wildly as the sure promise of another summer— the beginning of a new year. Great bonfires were lighted on the icy hilltops. Huge yule logs burned in the fireplaces of the chieftains' houses. The hearths in every hut roared with heat and light. Bards wandered from village to village, singing, under the flickering glare of torches, ballads about the old Norse heroes pushing back the wintry night.

In the Southlands, among the more cultured Romans and Greeks, winter solstice was celebrated with illuminations, feasts and orgies. In Persia the Zoroastrians worshiped light in the person of Mithras, god of flame. Sacred fires were kindled to him during his festival, the Mithrakana.

Prudently, the early church fathers did not attempt to abolish at once these ancient winter-solstice customs. Instead, by tolerantly absorbing them into the festival of the Christ Mass, they embraced and purified them.

This came about in the year A.D. 386 when the Christian emperor, Flavius Julian, fixed the date of the nativity festival on December 25. The emperor knew well, of course, that this date occurs only three or four days after the winter solstice, when the ancient pagan revelries began. Not being able to verify the specific date when Jesus was born, Emperor Julian sagely chose a useful date.

Then, because the Christmas festival arrived amid the dreariest days of the year, illuminations and the decorative use of light—candles, flares, bonfires, torch parades—became first indispensable, later traditional.

For a good many centuries this continued without much change. Then one December day in the sixteenth century, Martin Luther brought into his home at Wittenburg a small evergreen tree. Mounting it erectly, he decorated it with tiny candles and lighted them, as he told his children, "to simulate the starry sky which glittered above the stable where Jesus was born."

Long afterwards, Prince Albert, consort to Queen Victoria, after visiting Germany, brought back to Buckingham Palace enthusiastic descriptions of the candle-lighted Christmas tree. Thus, under royal sanction, the Christmas tree with its lights invaded England.

Meanwhile, hundreds of thousands of German immigrants were thronging into America. With them came a vast progeny of Luther's first Christmas tree, replete with toys and lights.

This cherished relationship between Christmas and light is not only ancient; it is world-wide. Christmas in the Southern Hemisphere today, despite its arrival amid summer sunshine, is never considered properly celebrated without candles and light.

Obviously, some deep truth nourishes this affinity. Let us mention in passing four national Christmas customs which distinctly emphasize this.

In Sweden for many centuries the adoration of light was focused on St. Lucia's Day, December 13, which ushers in the Christmas season.

On the morning of St. Lucia's Day, a girl in each household, previously chosen for the role, comes down the stairs or through the parlor doorway, while the family affectionately admires her. Dressed in white, wearing in her hair a cardboard halo, glorious with burning candles, she is St. Lucia for the day.

In rural France on Christmas Eve, in many families the father and eldest son, dressed in their holiday clothes, triumphantly carry into their cottage a newly cut log. Three times they circle the living room in honor of the Holy Trinity before depositing the Noel log upon the hearth. Reverently it is then lighted by a brand saved from last year's log. A moment of silence and tenderness falls across the household as the wood kindles and blazes up bravely: living emblem of the divine light, born to earth in a tiny Babe at Bethlehem long ago.

The beauty of the Alpine out-of-doors dominates the Bavarian Christmas, because Bavarian life is deeply tinged by mountains and forests. In many villages in southern Germany and Austria, Christmas Eve finds hardy mountaineers climbing the steeps, each towards his secret rendezvous, well prepared in advance. Below, the villagers wait in the snow and watch. Half an hour before midnight, suddenly the mountains thunder with explosions from mortars and bombs, and instantly along the skyline there flares forth a sea of fireworks. On the higher peaks bonfires blaze up. Every adult and child laughs and rejoices. The tumult and the lights subside. Then at midnight the church bells peal across the mountain valleys, summoning all to Christmas mass. The crowds turn to worship.

Not so quaintly, perhaps, but in our own way just as authoritatively and as beautifully, the people of the United States also mark the nativity season with a splendor of lights. All across this broad land every night during Christmastide there blaze out literally billions of colored electric lights. I have seen them from an airplane soaring by night through the chilly upper air. I have counted them flitting past train windows. During cross-country motor trips I have noted them everywhere—amid palm trees of California and snows of New England.

Considered objectively, it is quite astonishing to discover that for one brief season each year every farm, village and city of America suddenly is bedecked in the gayest and most garish incandescence imaginable.

Lights! Lights! Lights! Everywhere glorious sparks of burning red, green, blue, yellow, white. Little Christmas trees shining in farmhouse windows. Stores dazzling with colored lights. Streets in business districts garlanded with elaborate festoons of light. Dignified city buildings—Rockefeller Center in New York, the Merchandise Mart in Chicago, the Country Club Plaza in Kansas City, the Denver Civic Center are the most famous, but there are many, many more—abandon dignity for one fortnight each December and clothe themselves joyfully in gorgeous, fiery colors.

Truly, Christmas has become America's gayest and most beloved festival: the one season during which nobody is ashamed to exhibit delight in color and light.

Consciously or not, all these radiant illuminations pay tribute to the birth of the most precious Baby ever born. In a unique and strangely moving way, these myriad Christmas lights across our land and around the world reaffirm each December the fulfillment of old Isaiah's prophecy: "The people that walked in darkness have seen a great light: they that dwell in the land of the shadow of death, upon them hath the light shined."

God Kept His Promises

General Eva Burrows
1991

If ever there is a busy time, it is Christmas. I read about a woman who was busy buying Christmas gifts and preparing food for her family's celebrations. Suddenly she realized that she had forgotten to send Christmas cards to her friends. She dashed off to a card shop, chose one with a picture she fancied and in haste bought 50 of the same type. She hurried home, quickly addressed and mailed them just in time.

What a shock she received some days later when, glancing at the few cards that remained, she read the verse inside. It said:

"This card comes just to say

A little gift is on the way."

All those disappointed friends are still waiting for that promised gift!

Fortunately, it wasn't like that with God's promised gift. He promised a wonderful gift to all mankind, and He certainly kept His promise.

Long, long ago the Jewish prophets spoke and wrote about that promised gift. The prophet Isaiah said, "For unto us a child is born, unto us a Son is given, ... and His name shall be called Wonderful Counselor, the Mighty God, the Everlasting Father, the Prince of Peace" (Isaiah 9:6).

Yes, God promised a gift to the world. That gift was His Son, Jesus Christ, born in Bethlehem, given to the world to bring peace, justice, freedom and good will among men. To make the world a better place. To show men and women how to live life to the full. To bring reconciliation between man and God and between man and man. And the gift turned out to be even more wonderful than the promise.

I recently listened to a program on the radio entitled "Promises and Reality." It focused on the United Nations, illustrating how the reality has proved to be so different from the promises made. Such promises as peace in our time and famine wiped out. And the reality? More armed conflict in the world than ever before, and thousands still dying of hunger in deprived areas of the world.

Yes, the reality is so different from the promise. It is often like that with mankind. "Promises, promises," we say, implying that they probably will never be kept.

How different with God. The reality is so much better than the promises.

To prove my point, let us look at some of the scriptural promises. Isaiah writes, "Behold a virgin shall conceive and bear a son, and his name shall be called Emmanuel, God with us" (Isaiah 7:14, NKJV).

That promise was fulfilled beyond our expectations. God sent His Son Jesus to live among us.

If God were to send His Son into the world, you might wonder where He would send Him. You might think He would send Him to a university, to be among the philosophers, the thinkers, the intellectuals. You might think God would send His Son to the parliament, to be among the law-givers, the politicians, the policy-makers. Perhaps you might think that God would send His Son to be among the bishops and cardinals of the Church, to direct the spiritual life of the nation. But God did not send His Son to any of these places.

God sent Jesus as a helpless baby born to an ordinary couple, Mary and Joseph. He grew up in a family, just as we do. He worked with His hands as a carpenter, and knew how hard it is to make ends meet. He understood what it is like to be poor. He faced all the trials and temptations that you and I experience. Then, in obedience to God, He became the teacher of the good news, showing people that He is the Way, the Truth and the Life. But He was misunderstood, mocked, criticized, rejected, and His enemies cruelly hung Him upon a cross. This shining, sinless man carried our sins and opened to us a way of forgiveness, hope and peace.

Then He rose from the dead and is alive today. By His Spirit He is with us. Whenever a person calls on Jesus Christ, He is there, and in His presence we can find power over all that would drag us down and spoil our lives. He helps us to be the men and women we want to be, and that we ought to be.

Jesus is more than an attractive personality in history, more than a great teacher. He is God, as well as man. He is Emmanuel, God with us. He can do for us what no other human being can do! Promises and reality? The reality is so much more wonderful than the promise.

Another of God's promises we read in the prophecy of Isaiah states, "The people that walk in darkness shall see a great light" (9:2). That promise was fulfilled beyond all expectation when Jesus said, "I am the light of the world" (John 8:12). The light of His truth and His ethical teaching has ever since illumined men's minds and hearts. Christ's teaching has been the greatest civilizing influence this world has known, and when people allow Christ's light to pierce their self-concerned minds, He brings life-transforming power.

For light not only reveals, it energizes. "In Him was life, and that life was the light of men" (John 1:34). Into the darkness of prejudice and fear comes the light of Christ to teach men tolerance, understanding and love.

Yes, the reality is so much better than the promise. When we stumble and fall in the darkness of our own confusion and muddled thinking, we can pray, "Lord, shine upon us," and He will light the way to sanity and security.

Another of God's promises from the prophet Isaiah states, "The Lord is coming. He (will) feed his flock like a shepherd and gather the lambs in His arms" (40:11). God promises that the Messiah will be a compassionate, concerned leader who will care for His human flock as tenderly as a shepherd cares for his sheep and lambs.

And the reality? So much more wonderful. Jesus, speaking of Himself, said, "I am the good shepherd ... I have come to seek and to save that which was lost" (John 10:14).

In this modern world, there are 101 ways of being lost. Lost in a world of frustrated hopes.

Lost in a meaningless existence with no clue to guide you. Lost in a world of cynicism, doubting the validity of what you see and hear.

Jesus Christ cares enough about us to rescue us from our despair and uncertainty, our frustration and fear. His intimate concern reaches through to us, and He leads us to safety—even through the valley of the shadow of death.

God's promises about the Christ child were more than fulfilled in Jesus' life on earth—and the reality is even more magnificent in our lives today when we claim those promises for ourselves.

No wonder the Apostle Paul could cry out with a note of wonder and praise, "Thanks be unto God for His gift beyond words."

Smile Through the Tears

Major Barbara Salsbury
1979

"Oh no, it's Mom!" the lanky teenager cried as he saw the ambulance turn down Second Street. The wail of the siren caused his heart to pound and his legs seemed to turn to jelly, but he ran with remarkable speed the two blocks to the Salvation Army corps building and bounded in the door.

My son feared the worst as he looked at the two paramedics working frantically over me. "She will be all right—won't she?" his frightened voice could barely gasp. They did not respond.

"Watch her head, don't let it flop," one of the men said. Quickly they lifted me into the ambulance, and again I was headed for a lengthy, painful experience in a hospital.

One does not realize the tremendous blessing of unconsciousness until those first few excruciating moments of waking begin to penetrate in unbearable pain. I had no idea how much time had passed when I realized that two nurses were gently turning me. Intense pain shot through my head, and I tried to open my eyes, but nauseating dizziness overcame me.

A voice that seemed to come from far away said, "Don't be afraid. You're in the intensive care ward. We'll take good care of you." I tried to protest that there was no way I wanted to be in intensive care. Didn't people go there to die?

Although I thought my words were quite clear, obviously the nurse did not. She looked at me sadly and said, "Try to get some rest now." I tried desperately to remember what had happened, but I was so confused and tired that I weakly gave in to the comforting sleep that overcame me.

The next few days were a continual nightmare of pain and intense vomiting. Gradually I realized what was wrong with me. I felt so defeated. "How could this be?" I thought. I had just learned to walk alone in June after suffering a massive stroke 11 months before. Now, it was just November, and again both arms and legs were paralyzed.

I tried to deny what had happened. I guess I thought if I ignored the situation it would go away. Deep down was the nagging feeling that I would have to face up to it eventually. I had suffered another stroke!

As soon as my vital functions were stabilized, I was transferred to the Indiana University Hospital Medical Center at Indianapolis. There I was placed in a special stroke ward. I couldn't believe the arrangements. Men and women were together in the same room, separated only by curtains. Since I could neither move nor do anything for myself, I decided to make the best of the unusual situation.

I had no idea how God would bless and use me there, even in those circumstances.

There were six patients in the ward, and the three on my end, Walter, Rosemary and me, found God very near during those days. His presence helped to cement our friendship. We had many long talks about His will for our lives, and naturally we did question why this happened to us. We knew that we were all in the same boat—we all had something seriously wrong with our brains. As we prayed for each other, we learned more and more how to take our tragedies and fight them to a standstill.

That ward could have been the saddest, bleakest one at the hospital, and I am sure that would really have pleased Satan; but what he intended for bad, God used and turned into good. Sometimes we tried to sing together and often the nurses joined in, perhaps a little off key, but it lifted our spirits, and we knew God understood.

The days were filled with tests to determine what part of our brains were affected. Some were quite painful, all were very tiring.

Often when the nurses were busy my roommates would feed me. Then one day the occupational therapist asked them not to. "Barb must learn to do it herself," she explained as she patiently strapped the special fork to my hand again. I never realized what a job it can be just to eat! Often I was exhausted after only a few bites.

On Thanksgiving Day, Walter and Rosemary were given permission to leave the hospital to spend the holiday with relatives in the city.

I was beginning to get a little depressed. Holidays are so special to our family. I had bought our turkey weeks in advance. When a dietician came to help me mark my menu for Thanksgiving, she asked if my family would be able to join me. Plans were made to have the most delicious meal sent up on trays. I'll never forget the happiness of that day as my family sat around my bed eating turkey and trimmings, and we truly had a Thanksgiving.

As the days went by I wanted so much to still be needed. After all, God had called me to serve Him! "Lord, how are you going to work this out?" I asked. Even before the prayer left my lips, He had an answer. The next day I was carefully loaded onto the cart to be taken from the ward for another test. It was difficult to make conversation with the technician because he seemed so depressed. I knew the Lord wanted me to be of some help to him, but how? After a few questions about the test, I commented, "You look so sad. Have you had a rough day?"

"You wouldn't want to hear about it," he sighed.

"Sure I would. Maybe I could help." It seemed almost funny. How could I help anyone? God knew the answer to that too!

The test was quite lengthy and the technician poured out the entire story. About a month before, he and his wife had a great opportunity to buy a huge old house for a fraction of what it was worth. After the deal was settled, they discovered that the house would have to be moved. They only had three children, so they attempted to sell it, but nobody seemed to need a house that large. They were convinced they had a big white elephant on their hands.

Before further plans could be made, his sister and her husband were killed in a tragic auto accident, and he and his wife were going to have to raise their nephews, Jason, 2, and Ryan, 1. The shock of the accident caused his father to have a massive heart attack, and he explained that he must also care for him when he was released from the hospital.

I was beginning to feel overwhelmed when he continued with even more. Only yesterday they had learned that his wife was going to have another baby. So the family of five would quite soon be nine.

They would be needing that large house after all! I prayed silently that God would help him to understand that all of this really was a part of His great plan for my new friend's life. Suddenly my own problems seemed small and insignificant.

"You're a Christian, aren't you?" I asked.

"I try to live for God the best I know how," he responded. "I want to get my family back to church. I really do need Him."

As he wheeled me back to the hallway, I told him, "I'll be praying for you."

"I'll be praying for you too and—well, would you pray especially for little Jason and Ryan?" He was smiling, but a tear trickled down his cheek.

The lump in my throat kept me from answering, but I nodded. I realized that there is nothing so beautiful as a smile on the face of one whose heart is heavy.

He touched my hand and said, "I'm so glad

God sent you here today."

I never thought I could say it, but I was glad too. "Thank You, Lord," I whispered, as I realized I still had a job to do.

A few days later, both Walter and Rosemary were taken to surgery. I never saw them after that, but I know we'll meet again, perhaps in heaven where there is no pain or surgery, and all our questions will be answered.

When my tests were done, the doctor spoke gently but clearly as he explained what was causing my problem. It was difficult to accept, and I don't know yet what the future holds, but I've

learned to trust the One who does.

I still could only move my legs and arms a little, but they let me go home for Christmas. I looked out the window at the softly falling snow, and breathed a prayer for those who couldn't make it home.

I sighed as I watched the twinkling lights on our tree, and I thought of my dear friends, Walter and Roesmary, and little Jason and Ryan. Then as my own children and husband hugged me close, I looked through tear-blurred eyes to the shining star on top of the tree. I truly felt what Christ had come to bring so long ago—peace!

God's Peace Initiative

General Jarl Wahlström
1985

Carols are an essential part of our Christmas celebrations. Would not the festive season be infinitely poorer if we were suddenly deprived of our treasury of Christmas carols? We all have our own favorites among that treasury, and various nations have their own carols.

There are some, however, that are sung in almost every part of the world where Christmas is observed. One such internationally known and loved carol is "Silent Night! Holy Night!" the words and music of which were composed as early as 1818. Another universally known but much older carol is "O Come, All Ye Faithful" (*Adeste Fideles*).

But there is one carol that is as old as the Christmas message itself, one that is repeated over and over again when the Christmas story is read. It is in fact a part of the liturgy of many Christian churches and is thus read or sung the year round. I am of course referring to the song of the angels that first Christmas night outside the little town of Bethlehem:

Glory to God in the highest, and on earth peace, good will toward men. (Luke 2:14)

Looking closely at that greeting, brought to the astonished shepherds by "a multitude of the heavenly host," we find that it can quite naturally be divided into three parts:

- Glory to God in the highest.
- On earth peace.
- Good will toward men.

Here we have three very brief stanzas, but each of them contains a profound truth.

If we were to ask people which of those stanzas interests them most, I am sure the great majority would go for number two. This is totally understandable. Two devastating world wars have been fought during recent decades. During the 50 years following the end of the Second World War there has hardly been a day without armed conflicts in some parts of the world. And in spite of many sincere attempts to lessen the tension existing in today's world and to halt the arms race, we still live in the shadow of the bomb. We still ask serious questions about the future of the world and of mankind.

Why is it then that the promise of the angels in the second stanza of their carol has not been fulfilled? The message of peace has been proclaimed in sermon and song for hundreds of years, and yet we must admit the truth expressed by one hymn writer:

But with the woes of sin and strife
The world has suffered long
Beneath the angel-strain have rolled
Two thousand years of wrong.
And man, at war with man, hears not
The love song which they bring;

O hush the noise, ye men of strife,
And hear the angels sing.

Could it be that in concentrating on the second stanza of the angels' song we have overlooked the first? Have we really given glory to God in the highest, or have we just paid lip-service to Him? Giving God glory must surely mean asking about His will, following His instructions—all to hasten the coming of His reign.

Have we not substituted some of our man-made texts for the first stanza of the carol: "Glory to man and his achievements!" "Glory to wealth and economic development!" "Glory to my own country and people and race!"?

Let us all confess our selfishness and hardness of heart and pray that we may indeed be peacemakers. "Blessed are the peacemakers, for they will be called sons of God" (Matthew 5:9, NIV).

Is it possible for human hearts to change? Yes, it is, because God has not turned His back upon the human race. He loves us still. There is a third stanza in the angels' carol, a very important one: "Good will toward men." God has taken the initiative for reconciliation and peace. He has sent His Son to be our Savior and Redeemer. One of the names given to Him through the Old Testament prophet is the Prince of Peace.

There are several translations of this third stanza, that in their own way stress the tremendous truth regarding God's peace initiative:

"Peace to men on whom His favor rests"

"Peace to men who are the objects of God's good pleasure."

"On earth peace, good will toward men."

Some time ago I visited a famous war memorial in Honolulu. Those who had erected this impressive monument had also inscribed some texts concerning the problems of war and peace. May I quote one statement with which I wholeheartedly agree: "The problem basically is theological and involves a spiritual recrudescence and improvement of human character."

A spiritual renewal involves a change of heart which can take place through faith in God and His Son, Jesus Christ our Savior. Have you experienced such a change in your life? Are you at peace with God and your fellow man? Are you a peacemaker?

Home of the Christmas Tree

Colonel P. E. Wahlstrom
1969

One of the best-beloved symbols that belong to this time of the year is the Christmas tree, the gaily decorated and brightly lit evergreen tree. In homes, schools, churches and public squares it has an honored place.

Have you sometimes wondered how and where this all began? Where is the home of the Christmas tree, and who invented it?

I do not promise to give you a definite answer; I doubt that anyone could. But I can pass on to you some tales about the Christmas tree and at the same time tell something about the tree in our days and in my part of the world, which is Europe.

The Christmas tree hails from Germany. There seems to be no doubt about that. But when we try to trace its origin in more detail, we find there are many differing accounts.

A much treasured tradition concerns the devout English Benedictine monk, St. Boniface, who in the eighth century completed the Christianization of Germany. He tried to lead the prevailing modes of thinking into Christian channels, and one of his ways of doing this was to dedicate the fir tree to the Holy Child. The pagan Germanic tribes had revered the oak as the holy tree of Odin. Now the humble but evergreen fir would remind the people of the nearness of God in Christ.

Another source traces the beginnings of the Christmas tree to the medieval mystery plays. These crude presentations of religious themes were enacted in primitive circumstances with simple props to suggest the setting of the play. In many of them a tree was featured as the symbol of the garden of Eden. It was called the Paradise tree. When the plays fell into disrepute and were forbidden, the Paradise tree moved from the stage to the home and became the Christmas tree, symbolizing Paradise regained through the birth of Jesus.

The Germans themselves seem to favor the tradition that the western part of their country, around the Rhine, more especially Breisgau and Alsace, is the home of the Christmas tree. A chronicler tells as early as 1508 of the custom to "take a green fir tree into the home" for the festive season. Dating the custom somewhat later, a German magazine answers one of its readers: "The first Christmas tree was erected in Strasbourg in 1605. It carried paper roses, apples, tinsel gold and candies. Candles came into use as late as 1757."

To me, it seems rather bold to fix such a definite date for a custom that could have been introduced in differing places at various times.

It is difficult to say whether the above answer can be reconciled with the widely held opinion that the German reformer Martin Luther started the idea of decorating the Christmas tree with toys, apples and candles. One can well understand that he may have played an important part in this. He took such delight in the Christmas message, and he loved children so much. One of the best-loved European Christmas carols was written by him for his children to perform as a play at Christmas.

Nowadays decorating the tree has been developed into a fine art with varying traditions and national trends. Some favor a gaudy, multicolored display, while others go in for a more arty, sophisticated line, all white or silver.

The old custom in Scandinavia in families with children was to decorate the tree in secret on Christmas Eve and then throw the door to the best parlor open for the children to storm in, gaze at the glistening display and live the first ecstatic moment of that year's Christmas joys.

From Germany the Christmas tree spread north, but it seems to have taken quite a long time to establish itself. It is stated to have been in general use in Scandinavia as late as the middle of the 19th century.

The Anglo-Saxon world received the Christmas tree in royal fashion. It was introduced into England by Prince Albert, Queen Victoria's consort, who brought it with him from Saxony. The year was 1841. America received the custom from German settlers, who wanted to celebrate Christmas as they used to do in their homeland.

From the home and church—or Salvation Army hall—the Christmas tree has moved into the central places of our cities and townships. In Europe these mighty community trees are often a gift from one country to another, thus helping to spread the central Christmas message of love and goodwill.

Stockholm has for many years sent a tree to The Hague in Holland. Edinburgh gets its tree from Denmark. The Norwegians send these tokens of friendship to Antwerp, Rotterdam, Reykjavik and, most famous of all, to London, to be erected in Trafalgar Square and lit amid warm protestations of the close ties between the two nations.

Helsinki, the capital of Finland, sends every year a tree to Brussels in Belgium. These are but samples. Many more trees each year cross borders and dividing waters to help make real the longing for love and unity among nations.

In many European cities The Salvation Army plays an important part in erecting and lighting the community trees. Perhaps the most noteworthy of these ceremonies happens in Oslo. It began as early as 1919. The then women's social services secretary, Colonel Othilia Tonning, was a woman of many bright ideas and of great energy in putting her ideas into effect.

Some of her supporters had seen the great Christmas tree in the Town Hall Square in Copenhagen and suggested to Colonel Tonning that something similar could be done by the Army in Oslo. She immediately set machinery in motion to raise a tree in the center of the Norwegian capital. Her advisers wanted to pay for the tree, but the colonel thought the City Council could well do that—and they have done so ever since!

The tree is lighted on the first Sunday of Advent and the Christmas kettle appeal for the needy is launched at the same time. Thousands of Osloites gather in the University Square. The Army band plays and the territorial commander speaks. Last year the president of the City Council spoke appreciative words of the Army's work.

In Amsterdam something rather similar happens every Christmas. The tree is supplied by Norway, and the Norwegian consul general hands it ceremoniously to the municipality of Amsterdam. Then, in the presence of the consul and a Norwegian delegation, the tree is handed over to The Salvation Army by the burgomaster or an alderman. The territorial commander switches on the lights, having said his words of thanks and made an appeal on behalf of the Christmas effort.

Similar ceremonies on a smaller scale are held in many continental cities and towns. Army bands and songster brigades or string bands take part. And so the Army, with the fir tree, is helping to usher in the season of rejoicing over the birth of the Savior Child.

Shadow Over Christmas

Lon Woodrum
1964

Christmas is a time for making music, a time for warmhearted words and gift giving. The gaudy lights twinkle in the trees. Santa chuckles around the world as if he knew some beautiful secret. A million bells ring, and a million voices say, "Merry Christmas!"

We tell the story of the magi whose camels rocked westward on the trail of the newborn star. We talk of angels dipping earthward from their high world, their music floating on the winter sky; of shepherds who heard the great, good news. We speak of a cattle barn with its occupants that memorable night; of lovely Mary, patient Joseph; of the Child—God's Christmas Gift to mankind.

We follow an old tradition, striking a note of joy at Christmastide. But in this time of rejoicing and feasting and gift giving, unless we are quite thoughtful, we may forget something!

We may forget about Herod!

Herod is in the Christmas drama you know. He isn't under the center light, as is the Baby; nor does he show up as clearly as the questing magi. But he stands over against the joyful scene, brooding and ugly. His dark shadow falls over the cattle shed; in fact, it falls far across the land like a wicked finger pointing at those who feel the king's evil power.

In our moment of ecstasy over the thought of God's face being revealed in a Baby's smile, our memories tend to flee the grim reality of the deadly prince. But soon the Baby will hurry toward Egypt, hugged to a trembling mother's heart, while the prowling minions of Herod hunt for Him.

Never look lightly upon Herod! Say that he never would have been remembered in history save for his attack on Christ, but say also that God's own Son had to run from him under the cover of night. Perhaps Herod isn't very tall in history, but at that agonizing moment he was monstrously big.

Who has not shivered over the account of Herod's destruction of those innocent children? And what was the occasion for this? A Baby was born whose name was the Prince of Peace.

The Herods of the centuries cannot abide competition. Fear gnaws at their hearts when the name of an opponent is mentioned. Herod was a man of war. He ruled by force. A Prince of Peace would threaten his ugly doctrine. Only one way did he know to meet an enemy—with the sword. And so doom was set up for those innocent little ones who lay in his path.

This is the philosophy of Herod: better to snuff out a thousand lives unopposed to me than to allow one to live who might endanger my power!

So at Christmas we ring the bells, make music and give gifts, and all this is well. We need to do this, not only because it lifts our souls, but because it is proper to commemorate God's great stoop to our needy world. But let us, in the midst of our merriment, keep a lookout for the satanic figure of Herod. He does not like our celebrations. They presage trouble for his reign. All this talk of peace and hope, all these warmhearted greetings—selfish force does not take well to this sort of thing.

Not only at Jesus' birth did the cruel shadow strike across the scene. It thrust at Jesus through all His ministry. Opposition nagged at Him like a prophetic note of doom through all the gospel story. The devil couldn't let Him alone! He met Him at the manger, stalked Him through Judea and Galilee, hounded Him to Calvary. He sneered at His every good deed, His every kind act, His every gentle touch. Herod cannot abide the look of God—and Jesus had it.

Sometimes we have a way of sidestepping the strong messages of Christ and overemphasizing His milder words. We underscore His positive statements—and they are many and immortal. But we forget that half of His parables end on a negative note. He was ever aware of the fierce thrust of evil against Him. He kept talking about His coming death. His earthly life would end on a Cross, He said. When Peter took exception to this, He answered, "Get thee behind me, Satan!" He wasn't fooled, even if some of His disciples were! He knew about the glory of goodness, but He also knew about the stubborn drive of evil.

Many have tried to do with Christianity what they try to do with Christmas: make it all wonder and light, with no disturbing sequences. Shut the ugly picture from the mind! Dwell on beauty. God is in Orion and in the rose. "God's in His Heaven; all's right with the world."

The first part of that sentence from the poet is so. But we may have cause to doubt the last half of it! It's true many things are right with the world—a baby's coo, a mother's smile, a good man's prayer, a godly life.

But something is dreadfully wrong, too.

It would take a thick book to record all the good things that happen on our planet, but it would take a giant book to tell of all the terrible things that happen. Antichrist spreads himself like a green bay tree. His fierce wings rage through the heavens; his iron feet roar in the earth. A million cries come up from bleak nights where he exerts his evil will on deluded masses.

Oh, no, it is not all light and joy and serenity, even when we pause to look on the Bethlehem star. And all our glossing over the hard, grim facts in the New Testament really changes nothing. The facts remain. Herod still stalks our festivities. You cannot talk him down. Wishful thinking does not make him go away. When we open our eyes again he is standing over against all our faith, our hopes, our optimism.

It is an unfortunate fact that men want a God they can use. Often He is thought of as a cosmic bellboy; prayer pushes the button and puts God into action for the one who prays. Who wants a God who demands that we utterly abandon ourselves to His will?

"Come unto me, all ye that labor and are heavy laden, and I will give you rest." We like that.

Granted, we do need much. We are poor, weak, wretched, lonely, desolate. We need comfort and hope.

But we also need to hear this: "If the world hate you, ye know that it hated me." Or this: "In the world ye shall have tribulation." Or even this: "He that endureth to the end shall be saved!"

What do we really desire from our religion? Do we want ease and plenty? Or do we want victory over hell? Have we thought to find that elusive thing, happiness, by garnering stuff from an indulgent Father?

Where do men find the triumphs of life? If you would find an answer, run through the book of Acts. No, walk through it slowly! Take it all in. Have a look at those people in the primitive Church. Were they having an easy time of it? What a ridiculous question! They were fighting for their lives—and sometimes they didn't win. James didn't; Stephen didn't. They were mobbed, mocked, hurt. They got in bad with the civil authorities. They landed in jail.

Herod's shadow falls on that book of Acts with dreadful force. Herod spirits tear the Church to pieces, trample it in the ground. But don't let that discourage you! There's another Spirit in that book, too. This Spirit gives believers a dynamic that is utterly quenchless.

And joy! Do you know where to find it recorded? In that same wonderful and terrible book of Acts. Music rings up out of prison. Lame men leap in rapture at a pauper's words. Victory shouts rise out from under the lash. Angels come to help men. Earthquakes march to burst jails. It's the most incredible book ever published, for in that book you find the spirit of Christmas burning brightly right under Herod's frown.

Herod is real. He is a deadly enemy. He never seems to lose his energy from age to age. But, then, so are the magi real, and the angels, too. And the Baby! He is most real of all!

Imagine! God in a tavern keeper's cow barn! And Herod prowling restlessly in his palace, disturbed by a rumor. His legions clatter in the streets. One word from the ruler, and they will destroy whomever he wills.

Herod will attack the dream of God. But let the angels sing. Let the magi bring their gifts. Let men rejoice. God has made Christmas. God is in the world, and He'll never be out of it—now. The light, striking the shadow of Herod, will never go out. Finally Herod will fall, he will be banished from his throne. A thousand Herods will come after him, and they will fall, too.

The true King lies in a manger. Long live the King! The world is His, and the fullness thereof. So sing!

Christmas Wisdom

Journeying far,
By guiding star encouraged
Wisemen asked one question,
  "Where is He?"
The usual lurid night spots
Winked and beckoned;
Weary flesh sagged as they
Lurched Jerusalem-ward,
On lumpy, bumping camels.
There was thirst,
And flies;
Sands blazing;
Long sighs of disappointment
At negations
Of their strange and stunning
Star.

But no one, nothing
Could beguile them
As they jogged,
Journeymen profound,
Persisting,
  "Where is He?"
Until they found.

Lord, I pray,
Draw me on Your star-lit way;
Let no alien interest captivate;
May my quest forever be,
In all I seek and sense and see,
  "Where is Jesus?
    Where is He?"
       —Sallie Chesham, 1987

War Cry cover 1987: Ferdinand Petrie

allelujah! Promised morn!

ngels sing! Christ is born!

onging hearts no longer stilled,

ongings now have been fulfilled.

very creature come, rejoice!

et all earth become one voice

ntil all men together sing.

esus Christ—awaited King—

rrived on earth—Oh, make it ring!

allelujah! Sing! Sing! Sing!

—Colonel Mary J. Miller, 1982

Child's Play

What shall we give this little Child
who had the mountains for His toys,
who scooped the valleys up like jacks,
sent them rolling, and bounced the sun
to the pinnacle of the sky?
Who intricately carved white flakes
and watched them lace the velvet sky?
Who bent the boughs like boomerangs
and flung them far across the plains?

What bauble shall we give to Him
who strung the purple drape of night
and drew it back with bands of gold?

Who made the kaleidoscope of stars
and twirled it deftly round and round?
Who splashed His bootless feet in seas
and sailed aloft the ocean waves?
Who carved the mammoth jigsaw world
and joined each continent with ease?

What can we give the King of life?
Give one pure-lit, eternal flame
wrapped up in flesh and bone.

—Lt. Colonel Marlene Chase, 1986

War Cry back cover, 1976: William Utterback

A Christmas Prayer

Reverend Billy Graham
1957

Almighty God, our Creator, our Father and our Redeemer:

We approach Thee in the name and merits of Thy Son Jesus, whom Thou wert pleased to send to the world for the sole purpose of reconciling us to Thee.

We thank Thee for projecting Thyself into history in the person of Thy Son. We thank Thee for His willingness to leave the royal courts of Heaven to identify Himself with wretched, erring, sinful mankind. We praise Thee that He triumphed over every barrier that would hinder the carrying out of His atoning errand. Devils could not frustrate Him. Satan could not defeat Him. Sin could not penetrate Him. Death could not kill Him. He proved victor over the world, the flesh and the devil, and He alone merits our love, our devotion and our reverence.

At this Christmas season, when men of good will the world over pray for peace, give us an awareness that peace cannot come to the world if men refuse entrance to the Prince of Peace.

May we realize that, though peace has its material manifestations, it is basically a spiritual thing. Before it can come to the world corporately, it must abide in men's hearts individually.

May we realize that in areas of our lives where Christ is given His due place, peace already has come. As He comes in, strife, hatred and evil take leave.

Help us at this Christmas season to put first things first. Grant that each of us may accept Him as the One who came to "save His people from their sins," for then, and then only, will we come to know the peace on earth and good will toward men that the angels promised.

Forgive us for seeking a man-made peace! Forgive us for crowding Thee out of our plans! Grant that men everywhere on His birthday shall fall on their knees in true repentance of their sins and like the wise men of old, shall cast the things that are most precious to them at His feet.

Comfort the sorrowing, relieve the distressed, strengthen those who are weak, bring healing mercies to the suffering and save those who are losing life's battle.

In Jesus' precious name we pray,
Amen.

Where is He?

General Bramwell Tillsley
1993

I don't suppose there is any time in the year when children ask more questions than they do at Christmas. How many days until Christmas? When are we going to get our tree? What are we going to buy for Mommy? Perhaps because over the years I have been answering questions, I thought I would like to have a turn asking one.

We often remind ourselves that the theme of the Bible, from Genesis to Revelation, is Jesus Christ. What is prophesied in the Old Testament was personified in the New Testament. The promise became a person. In the light of this I

would like to link one of the first questions of the Old Testament with the first question in the New Testament.

In Genesis 3:9 God asked a question of Adam, that I believe demands an answer from all of us. "Adam, where are you?" Where are we, spiritually speaking? Our response depends upon our answer to the first question of the New Testament, the question posed by the wise men. They had been attracted by the star in the east and had been led to Jerusalem. There was but one question upon their lips: Where is He? "Where is He that is born King of the Jews?" (Matthew 2:2). They didn't simply ask for a baby but for a king. This was the spirit of those who had prophesied His coming. "And thou, Bethlehem, in the land of Judah, are not the least among the princes of Judah: for out of thee shall come a governor, that shall rule my people Israel" (Matthew 2:6).

With all the sentimentality attached to Christmas, this it the message we need to hear. Jesus is King and ultimately He will rule without a rival. "For unto us a child is born; unto us a son is given; and the government shall be on His shoulders" (Isaiah 9:6). The wise men were sure of His kingship, but where is He as far as we are concerned? If we believe in a sovereign God, we should allow Him to be sovereign.

A most significant statement referring to the wise men is recorded in Matthew 2:11: "On coming to the house, they saw the child with his mother Mary, and they bowed down and worshiped him. Then they opened their treasures and presented him with gifts of gold and incense and myrrh" (NIV). They had traveled many miles over many weeks, with the express purpose of presenting their gifts. But when they came into His presence, "they fell down and worshiped him." They recognized that He was born a King.

Throughout the Christmas season we will sing such carols as "Joy to the world, the Lord is come" or "O come let us adore Him, Christ the Lord." The word "Lord" carries with it tremendous significance. It means that Jesus is supreme and without a rival. In Revelation 19:16, He is described as "KING OF KINGS AND LORD OF LORDS." This is an objective fact whether we recognize Him as such or not. However, to exclaim with Thomas, "My Lord and my God" means that every relationship in life is secondary to my relationship to Him.

The apostle Paul looked forward to the day when Jesus would be acknowledged as Lord, "That at the name of Jesus every knee should bow ... And that every tongue should confess that Jesus Christ is Lord" (Philippians 2:10, 11).

O that with yonder sacred throng
We at his feet may fall;
Join in the everlasting song
And crown him Lord of all.

But Jude 25 indicates this should take place now. "To the only wise God our Savior be glory and majesty, dominion and power both now and ever." Jesus should receive the supreme loyalty of our lives, the supreme devotion of our hearts now. He should reign without a rival now.

May I suggest that at this special time of the year we take the time again to consider the direct link between our two questions: Where is He? Where are you? We should then bring them together as, in a spirit of worship, we exclaim:

The Lord is King! I own His power,
His right to rule each day and hour.
I own His claim on heart and will,
and His demands I would fulfill.

Dr. J. Oldham was surely right when he wrote: "There are some things in life, and they may be important things, that we cannot know by research or reflection, but only by committing ourselves."

O come, let us adore Him,
Christ the Lord.

God's Christmas Gift

Don Pitt
1965

Memory is a miracle—especially if you are deprived for awhile of books and papers. You can recall page after page of "The Christmas Carol" or important fragments of your earliest experiences. One Christmas, in much the same way, bits of things I had read and heard over a long period of time about a magical personality moved through my memory with astonishing clarity. One of the names I recalled was Eva. I was finding that isolation from books was a sharp disappointment, and I resolved that when I could, I would ask more questions, turn more pages and try to piece together the whole story. When I had done it, I thought it was a pity that Dickens had not lived long enough to write about Eva and her family, whose story began something like this ...

Eva was not born into a pretty world. Not that it was totally without a certain Christmas-card glitter, particularly in England, where tradition had built the season into a time of tender beauty. But underneath and close at hand, the world surrounding her was poor, harsh and bitter; and her father knew this fact as few others did, often feeling its influence within his own family circle. During a certain winter, Christmas shopping was relatively simple for a man with a slim purse, a consuming conviction and a family of six all claiming his attention. On this particular Christmas morning he brought his children a surpassing gift.

The day was almost precisely as Dickens might have described it. Snow, deep and still, lay on the doorsill; and in the parlor, six children celebrated the festivities as only children can. The door opened and a thin, pale, restless man, wearing a long coat and dark beard that doubled his age, entered. Steel-gray eyes, firm aquiline nose and jet black hair drew the eyes of all in the room to him—until they looked closer and saw in his arms a small basket.

Within the basket was a very tiny newborn child—Evangeline. She was the family's Christmas gift that winter. Or, as her father stated, "Here is God's Christmas gift." For years her brother Bramwell chided her good naturedly about starting life in a Christmas basket—unaware that such a basket would one day become as much a symbol of Christmas as holly, mistletoe and the gaily lighted yuletide tree.

The child-world which Eva entered was a protected one which William and Catherine had surrounded with moral safeguards, yet it was a world of joy and lively activity. Eva and her brothers and sisters were encouraged to keep pets: rabbits, guinea pigs, birds, mice and dogs helped make home a fascinating shambles.

Eva loved animals, and they returned her love, notably the marmoset monkey she dressed in the uniform of her father's Army until one day her mother gently suggested that it was all very well, but "Eva, your marmoset does not live the life!"

Besides animals, Eva loved the outdoors—field, forest and singing birds. Her days were not enlivened with movies, radio, telephone, automobile, Sunday comics or television. But she and her brothers and sisters enjoyed tennis and cricket, with Eva's vigor as batsman a family hall-

mark. No parlor games for them. High spirits kept life moving too swiftly for that, and there were few lulls, little quiet. Wisely, her mother—allergic to noise—had her sanctum, too: a room above, with a double floor between, packed with sawdust to deaden the wild tumult. Father was tidy, punctual and contemplative; and the children were not often able to recruit him in their fun, especially at the end of arduous preaching missions. But when he did join them, it was usually in a rollicking game of fox-and-geese, with William leading the chase.

Sundays for Eva were relatively quiet, centering chiefly around a Noah's Ark of ancient origin, its large biblical menagerie reserved for dignified, "instructive" Sunday play, with animals parading on a table, showing signs of wear and decay—especially in the lower limbs. Eva and her brothers and sisters gravely selected animals for sacrifice—though not according to biblical injunction, which called for animals without blemish. Those Eva sacrificed were chosen mainly because they could no longer stand up straight and bear the burden of the Sunday procession.

There was Sunday music also—piano, violin, concertinas and lively singing—plus "meeting time" in the play room, with Eva's sermons to a congregation of mops, cushions and dolls winning her early fame from among those who watched unobserved from their various hidden stations.

And always for Eva there was Christmas, a day of special significance for William and Catherine because it was not only the Savior's birthday but also Evangeline's—lively, witty, provocative Eva, who remained one of the family's brightest gifts which succeeding Christmases seem never to have surpassed. But one Christmas came very close to the mark.

William and Catherine, with their very excited brood, were gathered around the festive Christmas board, spread with such fare as an English family of moderate means could manage.

William's deep-set eyes were concentrated on his strong hands as they carved the Christmas goose; and when the children were not sniffing the plum pudding odors wafted in from the kitchen, they were watching their father's eloquent black beard with deep fascination. It always was a key to his moods, and today its wag seemed to promise total joy, which promise the children reflected back with the merriment of their eyes.

Not for long though. Eva's roving eyes had caught another sight in the dining-room window. The central pane was partially snow-covered, but she saw that a vigorous, unmittened hand had scrubbed the start of a peep-hole which grew steadily until it framed the face of a little girl about ten years old. Her features were thin and wan, her hair uncombed, her clothes drab and shoddy; and the frosty air seemed to have left pinch marks on her cheeks. But the little girl's eyes were eloquently large and spoke worlds to Eva. If ever there was a hungry child on Christmas Day, here was its personification.

Eva took in the problem at a glance. Generous, kind, impulsive, she darted to her father's side and asked permission to open the door to a small guest. He appraised the dinner table silently, and the children could almost see him tabulating each morsel. A look of uncertainty crossed his face.

"It's all right, Father," Eva interrupted. "I'll go without mine. Please?"

She had hardly realized until now the weight of her decision. Moments before her mouth had fairly watered, and its tastebuds were fully aroused. Yet Eva left her place and opened the door to the stranger. The hungry girl stood uncertainly in the doorway, dusting the powdery snow from her shoulders, taking a swift glance over her shoulder into the street as though she feared intervention at the crucial moment. Then she walked decisively into the bright room.

Eva seated the child in her own place, next to Bramwell; then she installed herself as waitress, ready to meet the waif's every wish. A princess could have had no nobler reception. The dinner moved joyously forward. Every morsel tasted doubly good because of the excitement a stranger had brought to the circle.

Another year passed, and once more the family of William and Catherine was deep in preparation for another Christmas—the double celebration that always made the day precious for Eva. This year William wanted to surpass all past observances. The intervening months had been hard, and he wanted for his family a supreme Christmas. A day of rarest happiness loomed ahead.

Christmas morning finally came. The family awaited William's arrival from his preaching mis-

sion. Somehow, his entry was always more dramatic than the advent of Father Christmas himself. But today he came in looking pale and haggard. He did his best to mask his feelings and tried to enter into the children's joys. But the discerning Eva noticed that he kept lapsing into silence and gloom, that his face remained white and drawn. Suddenly he stopped the joyous activity with an upraised hand.

"I'll never have a Christmas Day like this again!"

The children, taken aback, moved quietly toward Catherine, who approached her husband with anxiety and puzzlement, until he continued, "I've been in the East End this morning." He was striding swiftly back and forth in the brightly lighted room, studying the faces of his children. "I've seen the poor again—they have nothing on Christmas Day but the public house! Nothing but the public house!" His eyes closed as he told of the sights, sounds and smells of the dreadful Christmas morning.

"Others see only the drinking. I see the poverty, misery and disease!"

The plight of London's poor had torn his heart.

That was the last Christmas Day the Booth family ever spent together. Compassion drove them out to the people for whom William yearned. On the following Christmas, the family scattered through the slums and distributed plum puddings, just one hundred fifty of them; but they were the beginning of The Salvation Army's Christmas observances that have reached around the world.

Eva's gift of her own Christmas dinner to a waif of London's streets became the first of many millions to be supervised by the woman who became commander of The Salvation Army in America and ultimately its general throughout the world.

"The Lord accepted our humble puddings," William Booth said of that decisive Christmas. Ever since, Salvationists have added the same ingredients of boundless love and selfless kindness. These have made Christmas special for them—as always it was special for Evangeline, whose Christmas Day arrival coincided with the birth of The Salvation Army. Both were born in 1865, and both were dedicated to the great circle of humanity that is still served by The Salvation Army throughout the world.

Heartlist for the Holidays

Captain Steven D. Bradley
1995

It was the greatest disappointment of my young life when I opened the package that Christmas morning. It was a bigger upset than Goliath falling to David or Dewey being defeated by Truman, or the 1969 Orioles losing to the upstart Mets who were in the World Series for the first time.

I was five years old. A large brown Tonka truck was top priority on my Christmas list that year. Everyone in the family knew it. When the large box with my name on it appeared under the tree, I knew it had to be THE gift.

It wasn't. I got something I needed that Christmas—a bathrobe—not what I wanted. This lesson in values came, as far as I was concerned, much too early in life.

The Christmas season can teach us a lot about ourselves. About our attitudes; about what's important, about giving and receiving, wanting and needing. Many of those lessons we learn growing up, and most of them, it seems, come through disappointment.

That's how it was on the first Christmas. The world was looking for a great king, not a helpless baby. Many searched for Him in palaces, but overlooked the stables. Religious and political leaders wanted a Messiah of prestige and power, when they needed humility. They didn't find Him in the company of kings and princes, but with shepherds and barnyard animals.

In their superficial search for happiness, they never looked beyond the visible. For them, Jesus' birth must have been a major disappointment.

The Bible tells us, "Man looks at the outward appearance, but the Lord looks at the heart" (1 Samuel 16:7, NIV). Because God knows our hearts, He knows that we can never be truly satisfied with things. "A man's life does not consist in the abundance of his possessions," Jesus said in Luke 12:15.

When we try to find fulfillment in money, possessions or power, we'll always be disappointed. But when we're willing to admit our needs and open our hearts to God, we can be satisfied. For it's in matters of the heart that our Creator works His greatest miracles.

This Christmas, put a new heart at the top of your list. Experience the miracle of faith in God, who promises to "meet all your needs according to His glorious riches in Christ Jesus" (Philippians 4:19, NIV).

Christmas on the Map

Bennie Bengtson
1959

For a month or so each year everyone in our land is made aware of the Nativity. We decorate our homes and churches in recognition of the season, and we offer special prayers of thanksgiving to God for His "unspeakable gift, Christ Jesus." The commercial aspects of the season are obvious, for every merchant lends a festive touch to his windows with holly and mistletoe, evergreens and tinsel. "Merry Christmas" is on everyone's lips.

It is tragic that so often peace and love and good will, so evident during the yule season, disappear when the page for December is removed from the calendar. Like the ornaments and decorations, they are packed away.

Yet in the many individuals in whose hearts Christ abides, His Spirit is manifest throughout the year. Their lives speak constantly and consistently of Jesus.

Another place where the influence of Christmas has been firmly established is on the map of the United States. Ever thought of looking for it there?

86

In Christmas, Florida, it's Christmas every day in the year. The inhabitants of this little central Florida town—population 35—keep a Christmas tree decorated on the village green twelve months of the year. Many tourists stop to admire it, for Christmas lies on the highway running east from Orlando to the Atlantic Ocean. Each December visitors journey there to mail their yuletide greetings and to obtain the unique "Christmas" postmark. Still others mail their cards and packages to Christmas to have them remailed. The little, one-room post office handles more than three hundred thousand pieces of mail annually, by far the most of them in December.

It all started back in 1835 when United States soldiers and the settlers in the area were fighting the Seminole Indians. They erected a log fort for protection on Christmas Day and named it Fort Christmas. A community grew up around the fort and remained, even after a forest fire burned the fort years ago. In 1892 a post office was established and was given the name of Christmas, the fort having vanished.

Maine has a post office named Christmas Cove, and in eastern Oregon is a lake called Christmas Lake. Noel, which signifies Christmas in French, is found in both Missouri and Virginia. And Texans put Christmas on the map in another language—Spanish—when they designated a village Navidad.

Very much a part of Christmastide is Advent, the period of four Sundays preceding Christmas, which marks Christ's coming to earth. Cartographers can place it on our maps, too, for it is located in West Virginia.

Bethlehem, scene of the first Christmas, was brought to America in name well over two centuries ago by the Moravians. They settled in eastern Pennsylvania, and on Christmas Eve in 1741 they gathered in a small, log house for a worship service. Led by Count Nikolaus Ludwig von Zinzendorf, they marched in singing an old Moravian hymn, "Not Jerusalem, Lowly Bethlehem." The words of the hymn so inspired them that they decided to name their settlement for the birthplace of the Savior.

The holly wreaths and other decorations that brighten our homes during the yuletide season are scattered across the United States, also. To the people of ancient times holly was the "Christ thorn," so called because legend said the crown of thorns was made from holly. Then, so it was said,

the holly berries were white; after the Crucifixion they became red, the color of blood.

Holly appears on the map in many versions. In Colorado and Michigan it is simply Holly. But in South Carolina it is Holly Hill; in Mississippi, Holly Springs; in Arkansas, Holly Grove; in Pennsylvania, Mount Holly Springs; and in Kentucky, Hollybush. North Carolina has a Holly Springs, a Holly Ridge and a Mount Holly. And Alabama has a Holly Pond and a Hollytree. There are many others, holly being apparently very popular whether used as a place name or as a Christmas decoration.

Many kinds of evergreens are used for Christmas trees in different parts of our land. The United States Postal Guide lists no less than six Evergreens, one each in Alabama, Colorado, Louisiana, North Carolina, Texas and Virginia. Only Kentucky, however, has a Mistletoe.

Northern sections of the United States can usually depend on celebrating a "white Christmas." There is Snow in Oklahoma the year around, but it is a fourth-class post office, so there probably isn't very much! In Arkansas there is a Snowball; in Pennsylvania, a Snowshoe; in North Carolina, a Snow Camp; and in Arizona a Snowflake. The last named has nothing to do with the snowflakes that drift down out of the sky, however, having been named for two men, Erastus Snow and William J. Flake.

The original Saint Nicholas, it is said, was a bishop in Smyrna in Asia Minor. He had a long, white beard, and when he went traveling, he always carried a bag on his back. Out of this bag he would take gifts which he distributed among the needy. By the time St. Nick had come to this country and acquired his American citizenship papers, his name was Santa Claus. By this time, too, he had become somewhat of a legendary character. And he's just as generous as his Old World ancestor, even to giving his name to an Indiana town.

That happened a little more than a hundred years ago, on Christmas Eve in 1852. There was a settlement centering around the Methodist Church, but it had no name. When the residents met in the church for their annual Christmas Eve program, they also decided to find a name for their town. One name after another was suggested and discarded as unsatisfactory. The hour grew late, and still no decision had been reached. Then the door flew open and a white-whiskered, roly-poly gentleman dressed in red barged in.

"Santa Claus!" shouted all the children present.

Their parents accepted this as a suggestion and promptly named their town Santa Claus. Four years later, in 1856, the government granted them a post office. Today, though the village is not large, Santa Claus is a second-class post office. Because of the unusual postmark, it handles nearly four million pieces of mail annually.

The Christmas story, found in the Gospels of Matthew and Luke, has left many names on the American scene. There are Matthew, Kentucky, and Luke, Maryland, which account for both of the authors. It was in the days of Herod that the wise men came seeking the Christ Child. Herod is a village in Illinois and there are two places named Wiseman, one in Alaska and one in Arkansas.

The wise men had "seen His star in the East" and were following it to Bethlehem. There is a Star City in Arkansas, so called because it is surrounded by five hills, the points of a star. Bethlehem, Pennsylvania, has already been mentioned, but there are six more in other sections of the United States. The Palestinian Bethlehem lies "in the land of Juda" (as stated in the KJV). A third-class post office in Wisconsin bears the name of Juda.

After the wise men had "departed into their own country another way," an angel of the Lord warned Joseph in a dream to flee to Egypt. There are no less than seven Egypts in the United States, and ten cities and towns honoring Joseph—two as Joseph in Oregon and Utah, and eight as St. Joseph, with St. Joseph, Missouri, being the best known and largest of these.

By an odd coincidence, Mary is also remembered by ten place names in the United States, two of these appearing as St. Mary and the other eight appearing as St. Marys.

Luke's Gospel declares that it was Caesar Augustus who issued the decree that "all the world should be taxed." It was this decree that sent Joseph and Mary from Nazareth, in Galilee, to Bethlehem. A town in South Carolina has the striking name Caesar's Head. Nazareth is a picturesque old Moravian town in Pennsylvania, and Galilee also may be found in the state founded by William Penn.

Luke records the story of Elizabeth and Zacharias as a prelude to his account of the Nativity. Ten American towns and cities bear the name of Mary's kinswoman—Elizabeth, New Jersey, perhaps being the largest and best known. In addition there are half a dozen variations with suffixes like city, -town, -ton and -ville. Zacharias left his name on Zachariah, Kentucky.

The Biblical account did not omit the humble shepherds, watching over their flocks by night. Nor have they been forgotten by those who settled America and named its communities. There are four towns, one each in Michigan, Montana, Tennessee and Texas, called Shepherd. And this does not include such variants as Shepherdstown—two of these, in West Virginia and Pennsylvania—and Shepherdsville, Kentucky.

There is something very wonderful and noteworthy about the season of Christmas, and this feeling is brought to mind all through the year by the names which, on the map, serve as beacons of the spirit of Christmas, guiding all mankind to the Savior.

Desire of All Nations

Commissioner Ernest I. Pugmire
1949

Stand on a hill and watch the ocean. Currents in the shallows sweep in like smooth roads. Cloud patterns are reflected like ink stains creeping across an emerald carpet. The wind drives the breakers inshore; ceaselessly casting their white plumes on the sands. This might be the arena where opposing forces beat to and fro. Yet under all the coming and going in the waters there is the dominant pull of the tide. Wind and wave have no power over that will. The waters are drawn back; they pause; they return. Rhythm rules the broken deep.

Watching the ocean of human affairs we are

tempted to feel that all is confusion; all life is a beating to and fro, without purpose or meaning. But deeper and stronger than all the destroying conflicts there is a tide. The love of God never ceases to draw because it creates man's desire for Him. We toss in the eddies of our sinfulness. But we are still strangely attracted to better things.

Thankfulness for an uneasy peace prevails in many parts of the world today, yet another Christmas finds the outlook as full of foreboding as a stormy sunset. There is color enough, but it has little comfort in it. The light that bathes the earth is red. One hears the voice of Malachi: *"For behold the day cometh that shall burn as an oven and all the proud, yea, all that do wickedly, shall be stubble ..."*

But the picture drawn in the last chapter of the last book of the Old Testament suddenly changes. Giving to us one of the most heartening figures in all sacred literature, the prophet begins to sing of the Sun of Righteousness, rising with healing in His wings. So it is with our world outlook. There is yet hope. The last word has not been written despairingly over our portals by an Almighty hand.

Though many trends give us great concern, it is not a fair indictment of our civilization to say that it is wilfully plunging into an inescapable abyss of self destruction. However alarmed we may feel, our faith gives us eyes to see the signal of dawn. There is still the Sun of Righteousness, moving with uninterrupted march through the night which has seemed to be engulfing us, bringing a new day of healing and rest—if we will fear His name. The Almighty calls, and though there can be no more communion in Eden there has been a cross raised to inspire our desire and so make us ever hungry for redemption.

Christmastide, when we think again of Jesus, our Redeemer, forbids the bleak bankruptcy of despair. Such stormy nights as ours have occurred before. But, by the loving mercy of God, man has survived them all. His grace and patience have brought man ever to the sunrise. Man's desire for Him has not utterly failed. The longing for escape from the morass of distrust and fear has lifted again the sunken head of humanity. The people turn to find the light, no matter how its coming may seem delayed. The universe desires peace.

The poets of the nineteenth century sang their lyrics of liberty. For them the last day of human folly seemed to be in sight.

He comes to chasten, not destroy,
To purge the earth from sin's alloy.
At last, at last shall all confess
His mercy as His righteousness.

The dead shall live, the sick be whole,
The scarlet sin be white as wool:
No discard mar below, above,
The music of eternal love!

Then again pride crashed to its ruin, taking with it the faith of our fathers, until the young men sang bitterly of shed blood and minds were twisted by hate as the deep night of war settled on our twentieth century. John Greenleaf Whittier and all his school were hurled with mocking laughter into the limbo of discredited visionaries. Yet today the scientists gather over their atomic secrets to admit the truth that once again spiritual values are emerging. God comes once more to His own. The desire of men turns to find Him. In His (God's) day (the Psalmist assures us) "shall the righteous flourish and abundance of peace."

The sin must indeed be repented. Dust and ashes of confession must be worn in true humility. There must be the burning fires of sorrow, of great weariness and disillusionment. But when God's day dawns, when love conquers in the human heart, then come righteousness and peace, and with them the joy of upward soaring of the heart to Heaven.

God is ever striving to inspire man's desire for Him. Every springtime, every healing of the sacred earth by the slow, sure hand of nature is a symbol of His intentions. Whether it be the flowers of spring covering the bomb craters; the song of the lark above the thunder of gunfire; or the softening of the harsh face of the worldling as he looks at the Christmas crib—all such gifts would turn us toward the truth that man's desire for God is fed by God's desire for man:

Jesus, Joy of man's desiring
Holy wisdom—love most bright—
Drawn by Thee, our souls inspiring
Soar to uncreated light.

Theirs is beauty's fairest pleasure,
Theirs is wisdom's holiest treasure,
Thou dost ever lead Thine own
In the life of joys unknown.

It was man's desiring which drew the shepherds of the Nativity away from their flocks on the dark hillside to the crowded city. The angels had "gone away from their heaven." Moments of celestial ecstasy were over. The heavens' curtains were closed on the momentary revelation of the angelic chorus. The night over Bethlehem became as silent and dark as any other since man first folded his sheep. The shepherds could well have fallen to dazed discussion of what they had seen and heard and could have remained on the hillside until the reality of their revelation faded into hazy speculation. But, as from above God had reached down to them, so from below, from the depths of their hearts, longing for a Messiah reached up to drive them from their post of duty down to the city to "see the thing which had come to pass." And because they desired Him, they found Him.

Desire sent the Wise Men out on the long search. They had seen the guiding Star, so their journey began, because they longed to find the truth which they had glimpsed in the heavens. So they came at last, with exceeding great joy to the house "where the young Child was." Shepherd and seer, scholar and servant, shared the same Gift.

"Drawn by Thee, their souls inspiring," and all men have this precious Gift. It is found in unexpected places. Explorers in the Antarctic brought back word more uplifting than news of the discovery of fresh stores of uranium. The Christmas spirit, they declared, spreads from pole to pole. While Christmas can reign, Christ can conquer.

We have seen in our own times how powerless are political and ideological boundaries to exclude the love of Christ from the hearts of men. "God's Underground," that exciting saga of belief enduring under white heat, tells how millions of faithful people throughout the world have kept alight the fires of faith and devotion.

Lock the churches, ban the books, strive to imprison the thoughts of men and still the desire remains to lead us on toward "life of joys unknown."

So numerous have been the poems of the Nativity and pictures of the stable and the coming thither of Mary and Joseph to receive the Holy Child, we might conclude that nothing more could be said with pen or brush. Nevertheless, every year new poems are written. Every year the artists mix colors and approach their easels. They begin their pictures once more, and then stand back, knowing that when all their powers are exhausted there is still something more to say. The half has not yet been told. The picture of Divine Love which came down at Christmastime is still incomplete. They feel, in the words of Dr. F. W. Meyer, the great preacher, that "every element of individual wisdom, virtue and love develops in intimate evolution toward ever-highering hope, toward Him who is at once their innermost hope, their ever-attainable desire."

This being so with the poets and artists, we ordinary men can take courage and work to bring more of the Christmas spirit of hope and desire into the world. We must not hedge this season into a "mine own safe, serene hearth-side" exclusive festival, but we must push the borders out until the crib at Bethlehem becomes for all mankind the pointer toward God and the vague undestroyed longing for Him becomes the joy of finding Him.

When we ask how we might have a share in this, let us look for a place to begin in our own familiar circle. Is there not someone for whom we can pray just there, someone for whom we can be a beacon close beside us now?

Gift in the Manger

Bessie Bortner Scherer
1975

Jonathan had come upon the gifts quite by accident. He had gone to the barn for his sled and had found it standing against the wall in the unused stable. But almost simultaneously he saw something that looked strangely out of place. The stalls were empty. They had been empty for many years, ever since his father had sold the horses and bought a tractor. Yet the manger was filled with straw. He was certain the manger had been empty, but even if it had not been, there would have been hay in it, not straw.

He went over, lifted the straw up in his hands and immediately saw the shiny polished bat, the white ball and the leather catcher's mitt. He had such mixed feelings of elation and guilt that he couldn't decide which was uppermost in his mind. In all the years since he'd been getting gifts, and he was eleven now, he had never gone hunting for anything. Christmas morning was the first time he had ever laid eyes on any of his presents. Now it would be different.

He thought of Cleason Frank, his friend on the next farm. Every Christmas Cleason went hunting for his gifts. Last year he had raised such a fuss because the gifts weren't what he wanted that his parents had had to go and buy what he demanded.

Now for one impulsive moment Jonathan felt he had to tell Cleason, for here in the manger were things that even Cleason might be pleased to receive. But the moment soon passed because he was picturing an even greater moment tomorrow, Christmas Day, when he would show Cleason the magnificence of his new things.

His mother must have persuaded his father to buy so much! His father usually worried about the bills.

Slowly he let the straw fall back on the gifts, arranging everything as it had been. With great reluctance he left the barn with his sled. It was ideal coasting weather. He pulled the sled out to the little hill that ran alongside the apple orchard and coasted down several times. Old Shep found him out and came running and barking behind him, raising a great ruckus.

But he soon tired of coasting. He felt he just couldn't wait until tomorrow, so he started toward the house, pulling the sled behind him, When he came to the lane, his father was waiting for him. "I'm going to get the Christmas trees," his father said. "Mr. Frank wants one too. Do you want to come along and help?"

Jonathan and Shep sat on the drag hooked to the back of the tractor. His father laid two axes beside them and then got on the tractor and headed toward the little grove of evergreens. There were very few trees large enough, but in a few years there would be dozens of them.

His father stopped the tractor and together they walked to the edge of the grove. "Which tree do you want, Jonathan? These two are about

the only ones large enough."

"It doesn't matter, Dad."

"Well, cut that one for yourself, and I'll cut this one for the Franks."

When they got back to the barn, his father said, "I'll take our tree to the house and set it up so you can trim it. You take the Frank's tree and, well, suppose you put it in the empty stable."

He trusts me, Jonathan thought. *He doesn't know I found the gifts.* And suddenly he longed to see his presents once more before tomorrow.

He dragged the tree to the stable door. Shep ran after him barking and growling as if he were dragging the carcass of some ferocious beast. But when he came to the stable door he stopped suddenly, letting the tree drop. He turned to Shep and said, "Shhh." Somehow he felt as though this were a holy place. He tiptoed in. Shep followed quietly. It was as though they were entering a church where people were praying. Quickly he went to the manger. Reverently he lifted the straw.

"Thank you. Thank you," he said. But to whom he said it, he didn't quite know. Perhaps to the Christ Child Himself, who also was cradled in a manger. He picked up the catcher's mitt and put it on. It fit perfectly. Then he put the ball in the mitt and showed it to Shep. Shep sniffed and put his tongue out to lick it. Then quietly Jonathan put the gifts back, covered them up and went to get the Christmas tree. He set the tree against the wall of the stable and, looking in the direction of the manger, whispered, "Goodbye, I'll see you in the morning."

He spent the rest of the day trimming the tree. He called his mother for the final inspection.

"It's beautiful, Jonathan," she said. "Now go get the creche."

Tenderly he placed the little figures under the tree, but when he placed the manger he had such a yearning to see his gifts once more that he knew his resolution not to look again would be broken.

He went to the window and looked toward the barn. Mr. Frank was standing by his pickup truck talking to his father. The Christmas tree was lying in the back of the truck. It was almost dusk. "Hurry, hurry and go," he said to himself. "I want to see my gifts once more. Hurry and go."

He started putting on his coat and boots. As soon as Mr. Frank had left and his father had started toward the chicken houses, he raced to the barn. He was so eager this time he dispensed with all ceremony. He quickly opened the door and walked in. But the moment after he saw the manger he knew something was wrong. The straw was disturbed. It stuck up in great mounds in places and was flat in others. He ran to the manger, taking out handful after handful of straw. Suddenly he was at the bottom. But he would not give up. He knelt on the stable floor and flattened each mound of straw with his hands. But there was nothing.

His first impulse was to run to the house shouting, "Thief, thief," until he was hoarse. He wanted to tell his mother that the priceless things were gone. Perhaps she would know what to do, Then he started to think. Had his father known he had found the things and taken them away to teach him a lesson? Tears streamed down his cheeks when he thought he might never see his things again. He picked the straw up from the floor and put it back in the manger in the same haphazard way he had found it, but he was not as careful this time. Nothing seemed to matter anymore.

He went back to the house, wondering how he could hide what had happened from his mother. Then he thought that perhaps it was she who had taken the gifts while he was trimming the tree. Perhaps she had wanted to save herself a trip to the barn after dark. For a moment he felt better. But the old fear still clung to him.

He took his boots off on the porch, clapping them together to allow the caked snow to fall off. Then he opened the kitchen door and set them in on the paper his mother had provided.

His mother had just uncovered a big kettle of vegetable soup and the kitchen was filled with the odors he loved. A pan of baked apples was cooling on the sink ledge.

"Were you coasting?" his mother asked.

"No," he said, going to the closet to hang up his coat.

"I'll bet you're hungry, aren't you?" she asked again.

"I—I guess so."

"You guess," she laughed. "Don't you know? Well, supper'll be ready in a few moments when your father gets in from gathering the eggs."

He washed carefully, avoiding looking his mother full in the face. He was thankful she was busy setting the table. He was glad too when his father came in and they could all sit down to eat.

There was never anything the matter with his father's appetite. Perhaps his mother wouldn't notice his lack of one, but he might have known nothing could escape her.

"What's the matter, Jonathan? You're not eating. You're not coming down with something, are you?" she asked.

"No," he answered.

But while she was washing the dishes, she dried her hands and came to him, laying her hand gently on his forehead.

"No fever," she said, and smiled. "Worried about something?"

He shook his head. He was thankful she had gone back to the dishes and his father's head was buried behind the paper, for he felt tears well in his eyes.

After the dishes were washed, his mother started making the stuffing for tomorrow's turkey. He always liked to sample it, but even this didn't tempt him. He watched television for awhile, then decided to take a bath and go to bed early, thinking that the night would pass more quickly. But he was wrong. The night seemed interminable. He got up several times and went to the window to see if there were any signs of daybreak. It had become warmer in the night and he could hear the water from the melting snow running in the eaves. One time he thought he'd sneak downstairs and see what was under the tree. Yet he couldn't.

When morning finally came he hesitated a long time, hating to confirm his fears, yet his hopes urged him on.

He made his way to the living room, shutting his eyes as he approached the tree, hoping by some magic that when he opened them the things he longed for would be there. The moment he looked he knew that the gifts were not there. There was an opened box with two flannel shirts, another box with socks and still another with a pair of gloves—all things he needed. At the side of the tree lay a big white kite. He had wanted one for a long time, but he had thought that some day his father and he could make one together. In all the years he had been receiving gifts he had never been more disappointed. He looked up and saw his mother and father in the doorway. He searched their faces briefly to see whether there was any indication of regret. But there was nothing. There was nothing that said: "We're sorry! We bought some lovely presents, but a thief stole them and this is all that is left." Now he knew beyond doubt that they had not bought the things in the manger. Everything they had for him was under the tree. They were smiling. He must say something.

"Is this—" he began and stopped suddenly. He had almost said, "Is this all there is?"

"Yes, Jonathan?" his mother asked.

He touched the kite and was amazed at the softness of the material. "Is this genuine silk?" he asked.

"No," his mother answered. "I think it's nylon. It's made from a parachute, like the one your daddy used when he was with the paratroopers."

"And do you know what the tail's made of?" his father asked.

Jonathan shook his head.

"Your mother's wedding petticoat."

Jonathan was deeply touched. He knew that it was a gift of love, and somehow he felt unworthy to receive it. Yet a bitter disappointment still rankled in his breast. Where were the gifts he had seen, the gifts he had all but worshipped in the mistaken belief that they were his? His mouth felt dry and he was unable to talk. He was glad when he heard a knock at the kitchen door.

"Come in," his father called before he knew who was there.

"You in the living room?" the voice inquired.

It was Mr. Frank from the next farm. "Why did he have to come now," Jonathan thought. He couldn't stand it if he started bragging about Cleason's gifts.

"Yes, we're in the living room, Mr. Frank. Come on in, and let Jonathan show you his gifts," his father said.

"A kite!" Mr. Frank exclaimed in a tone that implied he thought it a strange gift. "That's as big a one as I've ever seen."

And suddenly Jonathan wanted to tell Mr. Frank, to brag about what he had. "Feel it," he said. "It's real nylon. It's made from a parachute like Daddy used, and I'll bet it'll go higher and faster than any kite in the country." Then he walked past them to the kitchen.

"Where are you going, Jonathan?" his mother asked.

"To try it out," Jonathan said loudly, to hide the catch in his voice.

"It's slushy underfoot, Jonathan. Not what you'd call good flying weather," Mr. Frank called after him.

"I'll manage. I'll—I'll manage," he stammered.

He heard Mr. Frank say, "Now there's a boy. There's a real boy. He really appreciates what he gets."

"How did Cleason like his things?" his father asked.

"I wouldn't know, Tom. I wouldn't know. He barely looked at them. Then he went and turned on television. We sure needn't have gone to all that trouble hiding his gifts in your barn. I might just as well have given him a stick and a stone. Yes, sir, a stick and a stone."

Jonathan stood still. The kite dropped from his hand. So that was it! That was where the gifts had gone. When the full meaning of the words surged through him, he felt a great injustice. Why was Cleason the favored one? Why did Cleason get so much and he so little? Why, why?

Then he heard his father say, "We've never had any trouble with Jonathan. He always appreciates what he gets."

Now he felt ashamed. He hurried to the closet to get his coat and boots. He must get out of the house as quickly as possible.

He had not gone far before he discovered that Mr. Frank was right. It was not good flying weather because of the slush.

He held the kite carefully. He must not let the tail drag. His father's words came back to him, *He always appreciates what he gets.*

Had he? Had he really appreciated the kite? He thought that he hadn't even thanked his father and mother for his gifts. Not only that, but he thought of how near he had come to saying, "Is this all?"

What about the gift in the manger—the real manger? Had some of the shepherds thought too, "Is this all there is? Is it for this we have trudged all the weary miles to Bethlehem, to see a Babe in a manger?"

He found himself crying. He didn't know quite why. Suddenly a puff of wind came and Jonathan released his kite—slowly and carefully. He watched it rise, higher and higher, until the string was almost entirely gone from his hand. It floated so high that it seemed to Jonathan to look more like a cloud than a kite. Now he felt such a sense of exhilaration that it no longer mattered that the gifts in the manger intended for Cleason were not for him. He knew he would cherish the kite more because it was a gift of love.

A Package for Your Soul

Commissioner Kenneth L. Hodder
1994

*For unto you is born this day in the city of David
a Savior who is Christ the Lord*

—Luke 2:10

Most of us feel that it is not enough simply to give a gift at Christmas. We want to wrap it to add elements of mystery and beauty.

But no matter how attractive the wrapping, it's the gift that counts. While concealment enhances the offering, the wrapping must first be removed before the gift is revealed. Following the process suggested by our Scripture verse, let us unwrap the greatest Christmas gift of all.

"For unto you"

Depersonalized giving leaves us cold. People in business exchange gifts at Christmas. Often the senders have no contact with the gifts, which were purchased in bulk by associates and automatically slipped inside envelopes on which computerized address labels were affixed. "That's that for another year," say the senders. End of the giving process—easy, quick and efficient.

But consider the Greatest Gift, who is Christ the Lord. The package is addressed "unto you"—the ultimate in personalized giving. And note the return address—the heart of God. The Greatest

Gift comes from Him. Furthermore, its declared value is "without money and without price." Its cost has already been paid by the Sender.

"Is born this day"

There is never a need for the Greatest Gift to be placed on layaway. It is always available now—"this day." The recipient does not have to hope it will come on time, or be concerned that it may not be available when the recipient is ready. The Greatest Gift is always available, especially now—the "accepted time." All the recipient has to do is to unwrap it. The Greatest Gift is waiting to be received.

"A Savior, who is Christ the Lord."

Finally, the Greatest Gift is revealed. He is the Savior. And He comes with this guarantee: if accepted, the recipient's past is both forgiven and forgotten.

The Greatest Gift's guarantee includes the opportunity to start living all over again, this time with a new heart and a new mind. At the moment of acceptance, the recipient passes from death to life and becomes a child of the Sender.

So where is this Greatest Gift, so beautifully wrapped and universally available? If you have not already received it, open the door of your heart. There you will find this package for your soul.

Where Has All the Good News Gone?

General Clarence Wiseman
1976

Frequently throughout history people have tried to create political and social utopias where everyone could dwell together in peace, plenty and goodwill. Some 19th century thinkers dreamed of a *universal* utopia, talking in

terms of inevitable progress made possible by the phenomenal advances of science. But such hopes were rudely shattered by the devastating events of our battered 20th century, now so swiftly moving toward its close.

Today the in word is *crisis*, not progress. Population crisis; urban ecological, economic and moral crises. Daily the mass media produce their doomsday diet. The whole world seems obsessed with frustration, turmoil and agonizing uncertainty about the future. One cannot help asking, "Where has all the *good* news gone?"

Mesmerized by this deluge of bad news, our generation seems almost afraid to ask if there is any hope, and where should we look for it? Somehow things have gone awry despite our good intentions.

And there have been many good intentions. For example, it was thought social engineering would edge us toward utopia. Vast housing complexes for the poor dot major communities in the western world; free health care has been provided in many lands; people have been cushioned against unemployment; children, the aged and handicapped are mercifully supported as never before. The intention behind such social actions cannot be faulted. Yet things still go wrong. Utopia seems as remote as ever. Bad news continues to dominate the media.

Is it possible we are afraid to confront reality, to admit that the bad news is really in our own hearts, that the ills that beset us are the ills of the soul? Environmental face-lifting and social improvement are good in their place, but they go only so far to meet the common malaise. They fail to touch the source of the trouble.

Some time ago a magazine examined our predisposition to blame everything but ourselves when things go wrong. The article declared that "people cling with their arms full of balloons to images of cherished innocence. They are willing to concede occasional errors, but not one of them will admit to what the sturdier clergy would identify as original sin. They prefer to believe that they live in a condition of almost perfect grace."

Too often we are reluctant to recognize that the solution to many problems and failures lies beyond the capability of computers, social scientists, even psychiatrists. Because *disease* and *treatment* are the fashionable watchwords of our time, we hear little of individual selfishness, guilt or the morality gap. Aren't we flying in the face of reality when we totally disregard the old-fashioned word *sin?* Isn't it high time we brought it back into circulation in order to match the truth of the human dilemma?

Of course, if we readmit the word *sin* into the language, it follows we are again face to face with *personal responsibility*, for sin is very personal even when it has far-reaching social effects. As a rule most of us do not like to admit that we are largely responsible for our decisions, actions and behavior. It is much less demanding to put the blame elsewhere.

Salvationists insist that the Good News of Christmas is highly relevant to all I have said thus far. We believe God understands how easily we are deluded into thinking that our modern cures will give us a good world, when actually they provide only a partial answer. The problem lies deeper.

We also believe that God knows how we would like to throw responsibility for our wrongdoing onto other people or upon our circumstances. It was because God knew we needed help that He came in the Person of Jesus Christ that first Christmas to live among us. He died for us and rose from the dead that we, through faith in Him, might be delivered from the guilt and power of sin! "God commendeth his love toward us," wrote the Apostle Paul to Christians in Rome, "in that, while we were yet sinners, Christ died for us."

The Bible is very explicit about sin, as you will discover if you read the first chapter of the letter to the Romans. And it is equally explicit about forgiveness of sin: "If we say that we have no sin, we deceive ourselves, and the truth is not in us. If we confess our sins, he is faithful and just to forgive us our sins, and to cleanse us from all unrighteousness" (1 John 1:8-9).

So the decision rests with us. We can go on sinning, living selfishly, lovelessly, in a world that has gone astray. Or we can come to God through faith in the sacrifice of Jesus Christ, and find not only forgiveness, but peace that passes all understanding and joy beyond measure. Such a decision does not mean we opt out of the world. Actually we become more deeply involved with people—loving them, helping them and never failing to give them the Good News.

This Good News of Christmas transcends the *bad news* of our times and shows what a noble and victorious thing life can become, even under the most improbable circumstances.

A Prayer at Christmas

Almighty Father, thank you for your Son, through whom you have made known your boundless love and truth, and your eternal nature. We stand in awe of the knowledge that through Jesus' incursion into time, you have determined that all creation shall reflect your righteousness.

We remember also, Lord, that the babe born in a manger will one day be revealed to all as king of heaven and earth. Though we see now but through a glass darkly, we ask that you make us able to give you the praise and honor that you alone deserve.

As your Son grew to fulfill His mission, we ask that you continue the process of regeneration in us, and make us able to help ourselves and others overcome loneliness, angst, poverty, temptation, blindness and hatred ... and bless your followers—who dare to proclaim you as the Alpha and Omega, the Prince of Peace.

And Lord, it is appropriate at this time of year to remember that Christmas is more than decorations and festivities. It is above all a time to recognize that you sent your Son into the world to save sinners. Thank you for the gift of your Son, Lord, and thank you for the birth of your spirit and life in my heart, a birth for which I and all those you have touched and will touch will be eternally thankful. In this world and the world to come, help us to forever exalt You above all.

—Jeffrey S. McDonald
1990

Artist & Author Index